SE AL

Will Eisner

Published by
POORHOUSE PRESS
8333 W. MᶜNAB ROAD
TAMARAC, FLORIDA 33321

FIRST PRINTING	1985
SECOND PRINTING	1986
THIRD PRINTING	1987
FOURTH PRINTING	1987
FIFTH PRINTING	1989
SIXTH PRINTING	1990
(EXPANDED EDITION)	
SEVENTH PRINTING	1991
EIGHTH PRINTING	1991
NINTH PRINTING	1992
TENTH PRINTING	1993
ELEVENTH PRINTING	1993
TWELFTH PRINTING	1994
THIRTEENTH PRINTING	1994
FOURTEENTH PRINTING	1995
FIFTEENTH PRINTING	1996
SIXTEENTH PRINTING	1996
SEVENTEENTH PRINTING	1998
EIGHTEENTH PRINTING	1999
NINETEENTH PRINTING	2000
TWENTIETH PRINTING	2001
TWENTY FIRST PRINTING	2001
TWENTY SECOND PRINTING	2001

Distributed to the comic book market by:
POORHOUSE PRESS
8333W. Mc Nab Road
Tamarac, FL. 33321
(954) 726-4343

$22.99 Paperback ISBN #0-9614728-1-2
Library of Congress Catalog Card Number: 85-61669

Printed in the U.S.A.

CONTENTS

3

4

FORWARD

This work is intended to consider and examine the unique aesthetics of Sequential Art as a means of creative expression, a distinct discipline, an art and literary form that deals with the arrangement of pictures or images and words to narrate a story or dramatize an idea. It is studied here within the framework of its application to comic books and comic strips, where it is universally employed.

This ancient form of art, or method of expression, has found its way to the widely read comic strips and books which have established an undeniable position in the popular culture of this century. It is interesting to note that Sequential Art has only recently emerged as a discernible discipline alongside film making, to which it is truly a forerunner.

For reasons having much to do with usage and subject matter Sequential Art has been generally ignored as a form worthy of scholarly discussion. While each of the major integral elements, such as design, drawing, caricature and writing, have separately found academic consideration, this unique combination has received a very minor place (if any) in either the literary or art curriculum. I believe that the reason for this sits as much on the shoulders of the practitioner as the critic.

Certainly, thoughtful pedagogical concern would provide a better climate for the production of more worthy subject content and the expansion of the medium as a whole. But unless comics address subjects of greater moment how can they hope for serious intellectual review? Great artwork alone is not enough.

The premise of this book is that the special nature of Sequential Art is deserving of serious consideration by both critic and practitioner. The modern acceleration of graphic technology and the emergence of an era greatly dependent on visual communication makes this inevitable.

This work was originally written as a series of essays that appeared randomly in *The Spirit* magazine. They were an outgrowth of my teaching a course in Sequential Art at the School of Visual Arts in New York City. Organizing the syllabus for this course brought into sharp focus the fact that during most of my professional life, I had been dealing with a medium more demanding of diverse skills and intellect than either I or my contemporaries fully appreciated. Traditionally, most practitioners with whom I worked and talked produced their art viscerally. Few ever had the time or the inclination to diagnose the form itself. In the main they were content to concentrate on the development of their draftsmanship and their perception of the audience and the demands of the marketplace.

As I began to dismantle the complex components, addressed the elements hitherto regarded as 'instinctive' and tried to examine the parameters of this art form, I found that I was involved with an 'art of communication' more than simply an application of art.

It is always difficult to allocate fairly credit for the assistance one gets in a work of this kind because much of it comes indirectly. To Tom Inge, who encouraged the idea of this effort at the inception and Catherine Yronwode, who contributed generous and thoughtful editorial support, my gratitude. To the hundreds of students I have had the pleasure of working with during my 15 years at The School Of Visual Arts, my appreciation. It was in the process of trying to serve their eager interest and learning demands that I was able to develop the structure of this book.

CHAPTER 1

'COMICS' AS A
FORM OF READING

In modern times the daily newspaper strip, and more recently the comic book, provide the major outlet for sequential art. As the form's potential has become more apparent, better quality and more expensive production have been introduced. This, in turn, has resulted in slick full-color publications that appeal to a more sophisticated audience, while black-and-white comic books printed on good paper have found their own constituency. Comics continue to grow as a valid form of reading.

The first comic books (circa 1934) generally contained a random collection of short features. Now, after almost 50 years, the appearance of complete 'graphic novels' has, more than anything else, brought into focus the parameters of their structure. When one examines a comic book feature as a whole, the deployment of its unique elements takes on the characteristic of a language. The vocabulary of Sequential Art has been in continuous development in America. From the first appearance of comic strips in the daily press at the turn of the century, this popular reading form found a wide audience and in particular was a part of the early literary diet of most young people. Comics communicate in a 'language' that relies on a visual experience common to both creator and audience. Modern readers can be expected to have an easy understanding of the image-word mix and the traditional deciphering of text. Comics can be called 'reading' in a wider sense than that term is commonly applied.

Tom Wolf, writing in the Harvard Educational Review (August 1977) summarized it this way:

"For the last hundred years, the subject of reading has been connected quite directly to the concept of literacy; . . . learning to read . . . has meant learning to read words. . . . But . . . reading has gradually come under closer scrutiny. Recent research has shown that the reading of words is but a subset of a much more general human activity which includes symbol decoding, information integration and organization. . . . Indeed, reading — in the most general sense — can be thought of as a form of perceptual activity. The reading of words is one manifestation of this activity; but there are many others — the reading of pictures, maps, circuit diagrams, musical notes . . ."

For the past 53 years, modern comic book artists have been developing in their craft the interplay of word and image. They have in the process, I believe, achieved a successful cross-breeding of illustration and prose.

The format of the comic book presents a montage of both word and image, and the reader is thus required to exercise both visual and verbal interpretive skills. The regimens of art (eg. perspective, symmetry, brush stroke) and the regimens of literature (eg. grammar, plot, syntax) become superimposed upon each other. The reading of the comic book is an act of both aesthetic perception and intellectual pursuit.

To conclude, Wolf's reconsideration of reading is an important reminder that the psychological processes involved in viewing a word and an image are analogous. The structures of illustration and of prose are similar.

In its most economical state, comics employ a series of repetitive images and recognizable symbols. When these are used again and again to convey similar ideas, they become a language — a literary form, if you will. And it is this disciplined application that creates the 'grammar' of Sequential Art.

As an example, consider the concluding page from the *Spirit* story, "Gerhard Shnobble," the story of a man who is determined to reveal to the world his ability to fly, only to be shot down by a stray bullet, his secret sealed forever by his pointless death. (See page 9.)

The concluding page depicts the death of Gerhard, as he is hit by a stray bullet from a shoot-out on a rooftop. The first panel presents the reader with the climax of the story.

AND SO... LIFELESS...
GERHARD SHNOBBLE FLUTTERED
EARTHWARD.

BUT DO NOT WEEP
FOR SHNOBBLE...

RATHER SHED A TEAR
FOR ALL MANKIND...

FOR NOT ONE PERSON IN THE
ENTIRE CROWD THAT WATCHED
HIS BODY BEING CARTED AWAY...KNEW
OR EVEN SUSPECTED THAT
ON THIS DAY GERHARD SHNOBBLE
HAD **FLOWN**.

9

A description of the action in this panel can be diagrammed like a sentence. The predicates of the gun-shooting and the wrestling belong to separate clauses. The subject of "gun-shooting" is the crook, and Gerhard is the object direct. The many modifiers include the adverb "Bang, Bang" and the adjectives of visual language, such as posture, gesture, and grimace.

The second panel concludes the subplot, and again uses the language of the body and the staging of graphic design to delineate the predicates.

The final transition requires the reader to break from the convention of the left-to-right sequence. The eye follows the air stream down past a nebulous background, onto the solid body on the ground; and then bounces back upward to view the half-tone cloud in which Gerhard is resurrected. This bounce is unique to the visual narrative. The reader must implicitly use a knowledge of physical laws (ie. gravity, gases) to 'read' this passage.

The accompanying text adds some unillustrated thoughts hand-lettered in a style that is consistent with the sentiment that its message conveys. The visual treatment of words as graphic art forms is part of the vocabulary.

TEXT READS AS AN IMAGE

Lettering, treated 'graphically' and in the service of the story, functions as an extension of the imagery. In this context it provides the mood, a narrative bridge, and the implication of sound. In the following extract from a graphic novel, *Contract With God,* the use of, and treatment of text as a "block" is employed in a manner which conforms to such a discipline.

The 'meaning' of the title is conveyed by the employment of a commonly recognized configuration of a tablet. A stone is employed — rather than parchment or paper, for example, to imply permanence and evoke the universal recognition of Moses' 10 commandments on a stone tablet. Even the mix of the lettering style — Hebraic vs. a condensed Roman letter — is designed to buttress this feeling.

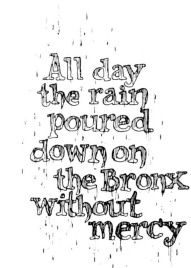

All day
the rain
poured
down on
the Bronx
without
mercy

The sewers overflowed
and the waters rose
over the curbs of the street.

Here, the lettering is employed to support the 'climate.' Designing the typeface to permit it to be drenched by the rain, converts the normally mechanical aspect of type into supportive involvement in the imagery.

Another example of how text rendered in concert with the art shows how the 'reading' of it can be influenced. In the following page from *The Spirit's Case Book of True Ghost Stories*, the dialogue executed in a certain manner tells the reader how the author wishes it to sound. In the process it evokes a specific emotion and modifies the image.

Compare this lettering style and treatment with the example on page 11. Here, the effect of terror, implication of violence (blood) and anger brings the text into direct involvement.

CHAPTER 2

IMAGERY

'Comics' deal with two major communicating devices, words and images. Admittedly this is an arbitrary separation. But, since in the modern world of communication they are treated as independent disciplines it seems valid. Actually, they are derivatives of a single origin and in the skillful employment of words and images lies the expressive potential of the medium.

This special mix of two distinct forms is not new. Their juxtaposition has been experimented with from earliest times. The inclusion of inscriptions employed as statements by the people depicted in medieval paintings was generally abandoned after the 16th century. Thereafter the efforts by the artists who sought to convey statements that went beyond decoration or portraiture were confined to facial expressions, postures, and symbolistic backdrops. The use of inscriptions reappeared in broadsheets and popular publications in the 18th century. Now the artists who dealt in story-bearing art for the mass audience sought to create a gestalt, some cohesive language, as the vehicle for the expression of a complexity of thoughts, sounds, actions, and ideas in a sequenced arrangement separated by boxes. This stretched the capabilities of simple imagery. In the process the modern narrative artform, which we call comics (and the French call *Bande Dessinee*) evolved.

IMAGERY AS A COMMUNICATOR

Comprehension of an image requires a commonality of experience. This demands of the sequential artist an understanding of the reader's life experience if his message is to be understood. An interaction has to develop because the artist is evoking images stored in the minds of both parties.

The success or failure of this method of communicating depends upon the ease with which the reader recognizes the meaning and emotional impact of the image. Therefore, the skill of the rendering and the universality of form chosen is critical. The style and the appropriateness of technique become part of the image and what it is trying to say.

LETTERS AS IMAGES

Words are made up of letters. Letters are symbols that are devised out of images which originate out of familiar forms, objects, postures and other recognizable phenomena. So, as their employment becomes more sophisticated, they become simplified and abstract.

In the development of Chinese and Japanese pictographs, a welding of pure visual imagery and a uniform derivative symbol took place. Ultimately, the visual image became secondary and the execution of the symbol alone became the arena of style and invention. The art of calligraphy emerged from this simple rendering of symbols and ascended to become a technique which, in its individuality, evoked beauty and rhythm. In this way, calligraphy added another dimension to the use of the pictograph. There is here a certain similarity to the modern comic strip if one considers the effect the cartoonist's style has upon the character of the total product.

In Chinese calligraphy the style of the brushstroke confines itself to beauty of execution. This is not unlike the style of a ballerina executing the same choreography as her predecessor but in a style that is, at once, unique and expressive of greater dimension. In comic art, the addition of style and the subtle application of weight, emphasis and delineation combine to evoke beauty and message.

Chinese letter or pictograph rendered in two styles of brushstroke.

Letters of a written alphabet, when written in a singular style, contribute to meaning. This is not unlike the spoken word, which is affected by the changes of inflection and sound level.

14

For the purposes of illustration let us follow the progression of a single expression from ancient usage to the modern comic strip. The ancient Egyptian hieroglyph for the idea of worship was the symbol shown below and which the Chinese similarly depicted.

Egyptian   Chinese

A rough example
of the effect that
'calligraphic' style
has on the
basic worship symbol
as might be used in comics.

In the modern comic strip the 'pictograph' for worship would be conveyed with calligraphic style variations. Through lighting or 'atmosphere' it could be modified in emotional quality. Finally, coupled with words, it would form a precise message to be understood by the reader.

Here the use of 'atmospheric' lighting subtly alters the emotional nuance of the 'worship symbol' in each panel.

. . . The underlying symbolic posture is given verbal and visual amplification. Dialogue, visually familiar objects (such as spears, architectural elements and costume) and facial expressions, convey precise emotional messages.

15

It is here that the expressive potential of the comic artist is in the sharpest focus. After all, this is the art of graphic story-telling. The codification becomes, in the hands of the artist, an alphabet with which to make an encompassing statement that weaves an entire tapestry of emotional interaction.

By the skilled manipulation of this seemingly amorphic structure and an understanding of the anatomy of expression, the cartoonist can begin to undertake the exposition of stories that involve deeper meanings and deal with the complexities of human experience.

This basic symbol, derived from a familiar attitude, is amplified by words, costume, background and interaction (with another symbolic posture) to communicate meanings and emotion.

IMAGES WITHOUT WORDS

It is possible to tell a story through imagery alone without the help of words. The following *Spirit* story "HOAGY THE YOGI, Part 2" (first published March 23, 1947), executed entirely in pantomime, is an attempt to exploit imagery in the service of expression and narrative. The absence of any dialogue to reinforce action serves to demonstrate the viability of images drawn from common experience.

16

The
postcards
used here
are meant
to convey
an element
in the story
that is as
"visual" as
the images
of people.
They are
only
peripherally
narrative.

Words like **"BANG"** are used to add sounds, a dimension not really available to the printed medium.

Symbols like **$** and **??** are used as thought rather than speech

The post card and the text on it is at once a symbol and a narrative bridge. It is important here because it is necessary that the rhythm of pantomime, a visual language, flow undisturbed.

The changes of scenery serve to convey location.

The rate of speed at which the action moves **'forces'** the reader to supply the dialogue. It is a phenomenon of comic strip reading that seems to work well.

19

Balloons, here, are confined to thoughts which are conveyed by images inside them.

Commonly recognized images taken out of familiar experience convey action (footprints) and time (the moon).

20

Facial expressions affecting the narrative require close-ups

The door label and the position of the hat suspended in the speed stream are narrative devices. The clock on the wall fixes the lapse of time.

21

In any pantomime, expression and gesture must be exaggerated in order to be read.

Speed lines indicate motion. They are part of the visual language.

Background art is more than mere stage setting, it is a part of the narration.

23

IMAGES WITHOUT WORDS

Images without words, while they seem to represent a more primitive form of graphic narrative, really require some sophistication on the part of the reader (or viewer). Common experience and a history of observation are necessary to interpret the inner feelings of the actor.

Sequential art as practiced in comics presents a technical hurdle that can only be negotiated with some acquired skill. The number of images allowed is limited, whereas in film an idea or emotion can be expressed by hundreds of images displayed in fluid sequence at such speed as to emulate real movement. In print this effect can only be simulated.

The intention in this sequence is to let the viewer supply the dialogue which is evoked by the images. The precise language is not important.

For example:

SHE: ''Oh, how my life is spent — ruined by living with you.''

HE: (. . . No answer)

SHE: ''You stupid fool . . . look at you! A weak nobody.''

HE: (Thinking.) I can't stand it anymore . . . her damn nagging.

SHE: '' Stop sitting at the TV day after day. You do nothing!! Nothing!''

SHE: ''Listen, I'm telling you I'm not going to take much more of this.''

This sequence from *Life on Another Planet* is yet another example of the narrative use of the image commonly experienced. Here, particularly because of the theme, with its demand for 'real' emotion and sophisticated interaction, there is little room for ambiguity in art. As in calligraphy the rendering of the line and the style of application attempt to combine a sense of character with the appropriate emotional ingredients.

CHAPTER 3

"TIMING"

The phenomenon of duration and its experience—commonly referred to as 'time'—is a dimension integral to sequential art. In the universe of human consciousness time combines with space and sound in a setting of interdependence wherein conceptions, actions, motions and movement have a meaning and are measured by our perception of their relationship to each other.

Because we are immersed throughout our lives in a sea of space-time, a large part of our earliest learning is devoted to the comprehension of these dimensions. Sound is measured audibly, relative to its distance from us. Space is mostly measured and perceived visually. Time is more illusory: we measure and perceive it through the memory of experience. In primitive societies the movement of the sun, the growth of vegetation or the changes of climate are employed to measure time visually. Modern civilization has developed a mechanical device, the clock, to help us measure time visually. The importance of this to human beings cannot be underestimated. Not only does the measurement of time have an enormous psychological impact, but it enables us to deal with the real business of living. In modern society one might even say that it is instrumental to survival. In comics it is an essential structural element.

TIME

A simple action whose result is immediate . . . seconds.

TIMING

A simple action wherein the result (only) is extended to enhance emotion

25

Critical to the success of a visual narrative is the ability to convey time. It is this dimension of human understanding that enables us to recognize and be empathetic to surprise, humor, terror and the whole range of human experience. In this theater of our comprehension, the graphic story teller plies his art. At the heart of the sequential deployment of images intending to convey time is the commonality of its perception. But to convey 'timing,' which is the manipulation of the elements of time to achieve a specific message or emotion, panels become a critical element.

A comic becomes 'real' when time and timing is factored into the creation. In music or the other forms of auditory communication where rhythm or 'beat' is achieved, this is done with actual lengths of time. In graphics the experience is conveyed by the use of illusions and symbols and their arrangement.

FRAMING SPEECH

The balloon is a desperation device. It attempts to capture and make visible an ethereal element: sound. The arrangement of balloons which surround speech—their position in relation to each other, or to the action, or their position with respect to the speaker, contribute to the measurement of time. They are disciplinary in that they demand cooperation from the reader. A major requirement is that they be read in a prescribed sequence in order to know who speaks first. They address our subliminal understanding of the duration of speech.

Steam from warm air expelled during conversation can be seen.
It is logical to combine that which is heard within that which is seen resulting in a visualized image of the act of speaking.
Americans call this a "balloon." Italians refer to speech clouds as 'FUMETTI,' thus, giving a generic name to their comics.

Balloons are read following the same conventions as text (ie: left-to-right and top-to-bottom in western countries) and in relation to the position of the speaker.

The earliest rendering of the balloon was simply a ribbon emerging from the speaker's mouth — or (in Mayan friezes) as brackets pointing to the mouth. But as the balloon form developed, it too, became more sophisticated and its shape no longer just an enclosure. It took on meaning and contributed to the narration.

As balloons became more extensively employed their outlines were made to serve as more than simple enclosures for speech. Soon they were given the task of adding meaning and conveying the character of sound to the narrative.

Inside the balloon, the lettering reflects the nature and emotion of the speech. It is most often symptomatic of the artist's own personality (style), as well as that of the character speaking. Emulating a foreign language style of letter and similar devices add to the sound level and the dimension of the character itself. Attempts to 'provide dignity' to the comic strip are often tried by utilizing set-type instead of the less rigid hand lettering. Typesetting does have a kind of inherent authority but it has a 'mechanical' effect that intrudes on the personality of free-hand art. Its use must be carefully considered because of its effect on the 'message' as well.

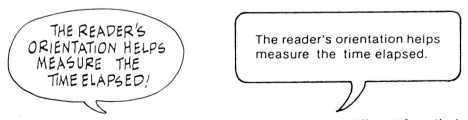

A hand-lettered balloon conveys personality that is quite different from that of a typeset letter. It also has an effect on sound and style of speaking.

27

FRAMING TIME

Albert Einstein in his Special Theory (Relativity) states that time is not absolute but relative to the position of the observer. In essence the panel (or box) makes that postulate a reality for the comic book reader. The act of paneling or boxing the action not only defines its perimeters but establishes the position of the reader in relation to the scene and indicates the duration of the event. Indeed, it 'tells' time. The magnitude of time elapsed is not expressed by the panel *per se,* as an examination of blank boxes in a series quickly reveals. The imposition of the imagery within the frame of the panels acts as the catalyst. The fusing of symbols, images and balloons makes the statement. Indeed, in some applications of the frame, the outline of the box is eliminated entirely with equal effect. The act of framing separates the scenes and acts as a punctuator. Once established and set in sequence the box or panel becomes the criterion by which to judge the illusion of time.

A MEASURE OF TIME

Morse Code or a musical passage can be compared to a comic strip in that it employs the use of time in its expression.

In the modern comic strip or comic book, the device most fundamental to the transmission of timing is the panel or frame or box. These lines drawn around the depiction of a scene, which act as a containment of the action of segment of action, have as one of their functions the task of separating or parsing the total statement. Balloons, another containment device used for the entrapment of the representation of speech and sound, are also useful in the delineation of time. The other natural phenomena, movement or transitory occurences deployed within the perimeter of these borders and depicted by recognizable symbols, become part of the vocabulary used in the expression of time. They are indispensable to the story teller, particularly when he is seeking to involve the reader. Where narrative art seeks to go beyond simple decoration, where it presumes to imitate reality in a meaningful chain of events and consequences and thereby evoke empathy, the dimension of time is an inescapable ingredient.

The time lapse here is predicated on the knowledge of how long it takes for papers to ignite and burn.

This extract from a *Spirit* story ("PRISONER OF LOVE" first published Jan. 9, 1949) deals with 'timing'. Here, the human action and a concurrent phenomenon (burning paper) are 'timed' to create suspense. The 'time' allowed to the fight is related to the time it presumably takes for the papers in the basket to burn. The shape of the frames also contribute to rhythm.

TIME ELAPSED

One minute

Three minutes

Seven minutes

Both of these critical devices, panel and balloon, when enclosing natural phenomena, support the recognition of time. J.B. Priestley, writing in *Man and Time,* summed it up most succinctly: " . . . it is from the sequence of events that we derive our idea of time."

The reader's orientation, the knowledge of how long it takes a drop of water to fall from the faucet, modified by the number of panels, helps measure the time elapsed. This reinforces the burning down of the fuse. In fact, one could even comprehend the time element without depicting the fuse.

In the following *Spirit* story, "FOUL PLAY" (first published March 27, 1949) time is critical to the emotional elements in the plot. It was necessary to frame a period of time that would encompass the plot. The problem was that a simple statement of time would not suffice. It would be too specific. It would mitigate the reader's involvement. A 'time rhythm' that is very believable had to be employed.

To accomplish this, a set of commonly experienced actions are used: a dripping faucet, striking a match, brushing teeth, and the time it takes to negotiate a staircase.

The number and size of the panels also contribute to the story rhythm and passage of time. For example, when there is a need to compress time, a greater number of panels are used. The action then becomes more segmented, unlike the action that occurs in the larger, more conventional panels. By placing the panels closer together, we deal with the *'rate'* of elapsed time in its narrowest sense.

The shapes of the panels are also a factor. On a page where the need is to display a 'deliberate' meter of action, the boxes are shaped as perfect squares. Where the ringing of the telephone needs time (as well as space) to evoke a sense of suspense and threat, the entire tier is given over to the action of the ringing preceded by a compression of smaller (narrower) panels.

In comics, timing and rhythm are interlocked.

An example of timing. Allowing two panels for the lapse of time prior to the dropping of the body, the element of shock, surprise and a bit of humor is introduced.

31

Here, the length of time it takes for a droplet to fall acts as a 'clock.'

Timing and rhythm are interlocked. For example, the sudden introduction of a large number of small panels brings into play a new 'beat.'

Long narrow panels that create a crowded feeling enhance the rising tempo of panic

33

The rhythm is **'staccat-to'**

. . . follow-ed by a long-stretched out panel to convey a long ringing time

34

Now, the pace quickens and the panels crowd each other.

Perspective is altered to add time lapse without altering the rhythm.

The rhythm is maintained by the use of narrow panels of equal size

The last panel, here, is wider to permit the 'beat' to pause a bit

Then the panel frequency resumes until the actor leaps through the window.

36

Now the 'beat' slows. Panels are more conventional.

The rhythm is slowed to a conventional pace. The story ends with a comfortable wide panel.

CHAPTER 4

THE FRAME

The fundamental function of comic (strip and book) art to communicate ideas and/or stories by means of words and pictures involves the movement of certain images (such as people and things) through space. To deal with the *capture* or encapsulation of these events in the flow of the narrative, they must be broken up into sequenced segments. These segments are called panels or frames. They do not correspond exactly to cinematic frames. They are part of the creative process, rather than a result of the technology.

As in the use of panels to express the passage of time, the framing of a series of images moving through space undertakes the containment of thoughts, ideas, actions and location or site. The panel thereby attempts to deal with the broadest elements of dialogue: cognitive and perceptive as well as visual literacy. The artist, to be successful on this non-verbal level, must take into consideration both the commonality of human experience and the phenomenon of our perception of it, which seems to consist of frames or episodes.

If, as Norman Cousins points out, " . . . sequential thought is the most difficult work in the entire range of human effort . . .," then the work of the sequential artist must be measured by comprehensibility. The sequential artist 'sees' for the reader because it is inherent to narrative art that the requirement on the viewer is not so much analysis as recognition. The task then is to arrange the sequence of events (or pictures) so as to bridge the gaps in action. Given these, the reader may fill in the intervening events from experience. Success here stems from the artist's ability (usually more visceral than intellectual) to gauge the commonality of the reader's experience.

ENCAPSULATION

It should surprise no one that the limit of the human eye's peripheral vision is closely related to the panel as it is used by the artist to capture or 'freeze' one segment in what is in reality an uninterrupted flow of action. To be sure, this segmentation is an arbitrary act—and it is in this encapsulation that the artist employs the skill of narration. The rendering of the elements within the frame, the arrangement of the images therein and their relation to and association with the other images in the sequence are the basic 'grammar' from which the narrative is constructed.

In visual narration the task of the author/artist is to record a continued flow of experience and show it as it may be seen from the reader's eyes. This is done by arbitrarily breaking up the flow of uninterrupted experience into segments of 'frozen' scenes and enclosing them by a frame or panel.

The scene viewed through reader's eyes . . . seen from inside reader's head.

Final Panel selected from sequence of action.

The total time elapsed here may be minutes in duration and the periphery of the stage very wide. Out of this, the position of the actors in relation to the scenery is selected, frozen and encapsulated by a panel frame. There is an unquestioned relationship here between what the reader perceives as the flow of events and what is frozen in time by the panel.

THE PANEL AS A MEDIUM OF CONTROL

In sequential art the artist must, from the outset, secure control of the reader's attention and dictate the sequence in which the reader will follow the narrative. The limitations inherent in the technology are both obstacle and asset in the attempt to accomplish this. The most important obstacle to surmount is the tendency of the reader's eye to wander. On any given page, for example, there is absolutely no way in which the artist can prevent the reading of the last panel before the first. The turning of the page does mechanically enforce some control, but hardly as absolutely as in film.

The viewer sees (reads) a film only one frame at a time. He cannot see the next (or past) frames until they are shown to him by the machine.

The viewer of a film is prevented from seeing the next frame before the creator permits it because these frames, printed on strips of transparent film, are shown one at a time. So film, which is an extension of comic strips, enjoys absolute control of its reading—an advantage shared by live theater. In a closed theater the proscenium arch and the wings of the stage can form but one single panel, while the audience sits in a fixed position from which they view the action contained therein.

Without these technical advantages there is left to the sequential artist only the tacit cooperation of the reader. This is limited to the convention of reading (left to right, top to bottom, etc.) and the common cognitive disciplines. Indeed, it is this very voluntary cooperation, so unique to comics, that underlies the contract between artist and audience.

In comics, there are actually two 'frames' in this sense: the total page, on which there are any number of panels, and the panel itself, within which the narrative action unfolds. They are the controlling device in sequential art.

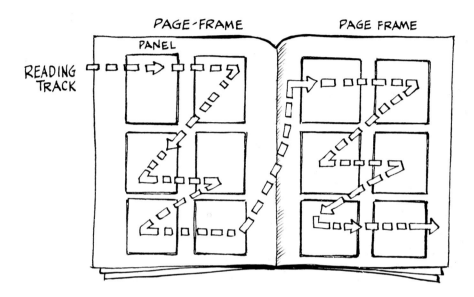

The (western culture) reader is trained to read each page independently from left to right, top to bottom. Panel arrangements on the page assume this.

This, ideally, is the normal flow of the reader's eye. In practice, however, this discipline is not absolute. The viewer will often glance at the last panel first. Nevertheless, the reader finally must return to the conventional pattern.

CREATING THE PANEL

In the main, the creation of the frame begins with the selection of the elements necessary to the narration, the choice of a perspective from which the reader is allowed to see them, and the determination of the portion of each symbol or element to be included in the frame. Each panel is thus executed with respect to design and composition, as well as its narrative consequence. Much of this is done with the emotion or intuitiveness embodied in the artist's "style." The understanding of the reader's visual literacy, however, is an intellectual matter. A very simple example of this is shown in the panelization of a single figure:

FULL FIGURE	MEDIUM	CLOSE-UP
The figure shown in full requires no sophistication. It asks nothing of the reader's imagination or knowledge.	The reader is expected to supply the rest of the image — given a generous hint of the anatomy.	The reader is expected to assume that the entire figure exists and to deduce out of memory and experience the posture and detail.

When the full figure is shown (A), no sophistication is required of the reader. The entire image is complete and intact. In panel (B) the reader is expected to understand that the figure shown has legs in proper proportion to the torso and that they are in a compatible position. In the closeup (C), the reader is expected to assume an entire body exists outside the panel and, based on experience and memory, must supply the rest of the picture in conformity with what the physiology of the head suggests.

42

In a given series of panels wherein the frame encompasses only the head, a 'visual dialogue' occurs between the reader and the artist which requires certain assumptions growing out of a common level of experience:

The slim head (A) implies a slim body.

The fat head (B) implies a fat body.

Subsequent views of the characters will of course substantiate these assumptions. Illustration C, however, serves to demonstrate that there can be a misreading of the artist's intentions unless a more skilled drawing is executed in the panel itself or a prior panel has established what it is the reader is viewing.

THE PANEL AS A CONTAINER

The most basic panel layout is one in which both the shape and proportion of the box remain rigid. The panels act to contain the reader's view, nothing

more. This type of 'panelization' is more commonly seen in comic strips than in comic books because it is a natural extension of the format requirements of the newspapers in which they appear.

THE 'LANGUAGE' OF THE PANEL BORDER

In addition to its primary function as a frame in which to place objects and actions, the panel border itself can be used as part of the non-verbal 'language' of sequential art.

For example, rectangular panels with straight edged borders (A), unless the verbal portion of the narrative contradicts this, usually are meant to imply that the actions contained therein are set in the present tense. The flashback (a change in tense or shift in time) is often indicated by altering the line which makes up the frame. The wavy edged (B) or scalloped (C) panel border is the most common past time indicator. While there is no universally agreed upon convention for expressing tense through the outline of the frame, the 'character' of the line—as in the case of sound, emotion (D) or thought (C)—creates a hieroglyphic.

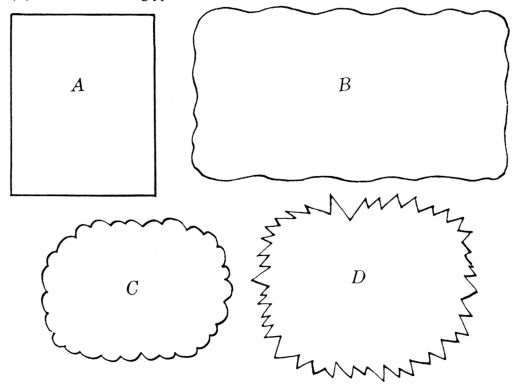

44

The non-frame speaks to unlimited space. It has the effect of encompassing unseen but acknowledged background. The following from a *Spirit* story, "THE TRAGEDY OF MERRY ANDREW" (first published February 15, 1948), is an example of this;

The carnival set not shown here was displayed in the story's earlier pages. The reader is required to 'fill it in,' now. On this page the open panels are intended to imply unlimited space and the suggested setting.

When all had laughed and passed remarks
   About how soft he was,
Our Merry Andrew calmly drew
   "...Five grand for him that does!"

Win more dough for the purse they had??
   ...And by a gloved combat??
Big and small and short and tall
   They all threw in their hats.

But Dolan thought he'd play it shrewd...
   Eliminate a loss;
He ordered up the Spirit, and...
   The ten-grand purse, of course.

The use of a structural panel frame reinforces the reader's memory of the setting

Non-frame — The reader again supplies the background.

45

THE FRAME AS A NARRATIVE DEVICE

The frame's shape (or absence of one) can become a part of the story itself. It can be used to convey something of the dimension of sound and emotional climate in which the action occurs, as well as contributing to the atmosphere of the page as a whole. The intent of the frame here is not so much to provide a stage as to heighten the reader's involvement with the narrative. Whereas the conventional container-frame keeps the reader at bay—or out of the picture, so to speak—the frame as used in the examples below invites the reader into the action or allows the action to 'explode' toward the reader. In addition to adding a secondary intellectual level to the narrative, it tries to deal with other sensory dimensions.

A. The jagged outline implies an emotionally explosive action. It conveys a state of tension and is related to crisp crackle associated with radio or telephonic transmission of sound.

B. The long panel reinforces the illusion of height. The positioning of several square panels emulate a falling motion.

C. The illusion of power and threat is displayed by allowing the actor to burst out of the confines of the panel. Since the panel border is assumed to be inviolate in a comic page this adds to the sense of unleashed action.

D. The absence of a panel outline is designed to convey unlimited space. It provides a sense of serenity and supports the narrative by contributing atmosphere to the narrative.

E. The 'panel' here is actually the doorway. It tells the reader that the actor is confined in a small area within a wider one — the building. It narrates this visually.

F. The cloudlike enclosure defines the picture as being a thought, or memory. The action would be read as actually taking place if there were no panel or a hard outline.

In the following example, a one-page segment from a *Spirit* story "THE EXPLORER" (first published January 16, 1949), the shape of the panel and even its rendering (such as a heavy versus a light outline) seeks to deal with distance from the front of the stage. As in the theatre we are dealing with actions that are taking place on two tracks of time.

In dealing with concurrent actions the formal (heavy outline) panel is used to contain the 'now' action and the non-outline serves to contain the 'meanwhile.'

47

The illusion of unlimited space is demonstrated by the eliminaton of a panel outline.

Three small panels contained by a thick outline superimposed over a broader panel with a thin outline are meant to convey a time-focus necessary to the narrative.

The absence of a panel outline here narrates the duration of time and the limitless locale critical to the story.

The hard outline of the last frame announces the close of the sequence.

THE FRAME AS A STRUCTURAL SUPPORT

In these examples the frame's outline becomes part of the apparatus for suggesting dimension. The use of the panel border as a structural element, when so employed, serves to involve the reader and encompasses far more than a simple container-panel. The sheer novelty of the interplay between the contained space and the 'non-space' (the gutter) between the panels also conveys a sense of heightened significance within the narrative structure.

An example of the use of a doorway or window which, while resembling a panel, is nevertheless a structure in the setting of the story.

The normal 'gutter' (space between panels) is actually expanded here to convey open 'desert' while the outline of eyes as seen from inside the head serve as panels.

In this extract from the *Spirit* story "TUNNEL" (first published March 21, 1948), the 'non-space' between the panels is literally the ground from which they are formed.

THE PANEL OUTLINE

The range of possibility of outline is limited only to the requirements of the narrative and the constrictions of the page dimensions. Because the function of the panel outline is in service of the story it is actually created after—or in response to the action determined by the author/artist.

Here is a series of panel outlines freed of their internal images.

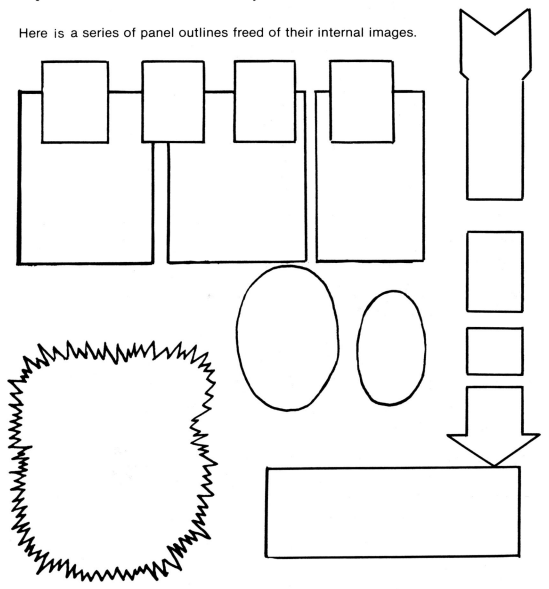

They were employed in the following Spirit story "THE AMULET OF OSIRIS" (Nov. 28, 1948) as narrative devices.

The arrangement of panel outlines and shapes on this page is devised to deal with the problem of reader discipline. The rhythm of the narrative is set in this manner.

This panel device is meant to direct the reader's eye toward the next panel as it relates events.

Here, the placement of a head, freed, but relating to the narrow flat panel, evokes a feeling of a page that has unlimited dimensions.

The door-way is the container in this panel.

The panel outline is actually the window frame. This is an integral piece of background art that tells of a shift in location.

53

The panel is outlined by an 'electric shock' simulation which serves the narrative.

54

55

An open panel that narrates space, time and location.

The use of an open panel here suggests the dimensions of the airfield.

57

The port-holes are designed to also serve as panel outlines.

58

THE EMOTIONAL FUNCTION OF THE FRAME

The shape and treatment of the frames in the following three examples deal with the viewer's emotions. They make an effort to generate the reader's own reaction to the action and thus create emotional involvement in the narrative.

EXAMPLE (A) In the sequence dealing with the Spirit's recovery from blindness, the view is actually from inside the protagonist's eyes. The panel outline speaks to this and hopefully enables the reader to share in the experience. From the *Spirit* story "FLUID X"(first published September 14, 1947).

EXAMPLE (B) In this segment from the *Spirit* story "DEADLINE" (first published December 31, 1950), the rippled edges of the panel and its oblong shape intends uncertainty and impending danger. It is directed at the reader's sense of 'feel.'

EXAMPLE (C) This treatment from a *Spirit* story "THE OCTOPUS IS BACK" (first published February 11, 1951), is set on a subway where the rocking of the train is meant to be 'felt' by the reader. Tilting of panels and lettering seeks to create the subliminal effect.

THE 'SPLASH' PAGE

The first page of a story functions as an introduction. What, or how much, it contains depends on the number of pages that follow. It is a launching pad for the narrative, and for most stories it establishes a frame of reference. Properly employed it seizes the reader's attention and prepares his attitude for the events to follow. It sets a 'climate.' It becomes a 'splash' page proper rather than a simple 'first page' when the artist designs it as a decorative unit.

THE PAGE AS A META PANEL

In the following chapter from "LIFE ON ANOTHER PLANET" (first published August 1980) the panel is subordinated to the totality of the narrative. The panel is, in the conventional configuration, used only sparingly. A synthesis of speed, multi-leveled action, narrative and the dimensions of the stage is attempted.

The problem here is to employ the panel so that it will not intrude on the segment of the story encompassed by the page frame. Thus for most of the story, the 'hard-frame' is not the individual panel but the total page.

Where the actors are displaying powerful and sophisticated emotions—where their postures and gestures are subtle and critical to the telling of the story—the panel outlines become a liability unless imposed with concern for their effect on what they contain.

One important facet of the full-page frame is that planning the breakdown of the plot and action into page segments becomes the first order of business. Pages are the constant in comic book narration. They have to be dealt with immediately after the story is solidified. Because the groupings of action and other events do not necessarily break up evenly, some pages must contain more individual scenes than others. Keep in mind that when the reader turns the page a pause occurs. This permits a change of time, a shift of scene, an opportunity to control the reader's focus. Here one deals with retention as well as attention. The page as well as the panel must therefore be addressed as a unit of containment although it too is merely a part of the whole comprised by the story itself.

In the following example, each page is of unequal reading duration, time and rhythm. Each encompasses a different time and setting. Each page is a result of careful deliberation. Please note that there was no intention to create 'page interest' at the cost of subordinating the internal (story telling) panels. If a rule is possible, I would ordain that *"what goes on INSIDE the panel is PRIMARY!"*

63

The entire page serves as a super-panel and as a splash page at the same time. The individual panels vary from small close-ups set on another plane to the overriding panel at the bottom.

The small panels float above and in front of the plane on which this larger panel is set.

These panels are the main action panels.

On this page a set of events not necessarily concurrent or in sequence must be held together because the threads of the plot are meant to be separate but related.

The event on the top tier occurs in a different time and place from the sequence below which occurs in a more confined environment.

65

On this page the super-panel contains a sequence of short duration. In reality it is a single unit that concludes the action begun on the previous page.

This page holds the reader in place while it permits a series of actions which have a flexible time frame. It is not a flashback or 'thought' panel . . . it simply accelerates the narrative.

This panel employs the steam from the shower as a connecting device and employs the super panel of the page to slow down the rate of narration.

The man drinking is positioned so as to introduce the panel on the next page. It seeks to separate itself from the page unit, leaving the integrity of the page intact.

Because of the fluidity of the action and the amorphous quality of the setting the page is, at first glance, read as a single panel. The dominance of the art at the bottom ordains this.

The page
acting as
container,
permits the
upper half
to conclude
the action
of the pre-
vious page
while the
two tiers of
the lower
half
dominate.
Because of
this, the
page is
seen as two
units, each
within a
fixed site.

70

Here, as on earlier pages, time and location are juxtaposed so that the page is first seen in totality. The details of action are the weave in the fabric.

Once again the total page functions to set mood, rhythm and climate. This is especially useful when there is fast-paced activity.

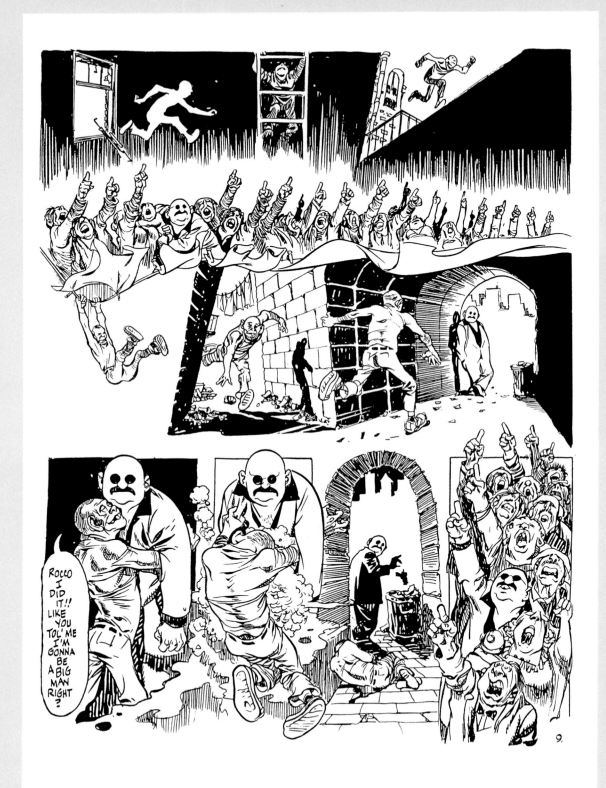

To deal with the ballet-like movement of the fugitive, the single background is used as a device to support two panels.

With an overriding background narrative such as the newspaper story — the page becomes a sub- or underlying panel by acting as an extension of the newspaper itself.

Another example where the page is to be a panel containing the major statement . . . that is the hero attacking the kidnapper. The rest are sub-panels or background.

74

This page attempts to deal with a major problem in a swiftly moving narrative. Within the broad action of an escape a critically important detail (the stabbing of the girl with an umbrella) is centered on the page. It is the best solution because it must have enough emphasis to lodge itself in the reader's memory. Obviously the girl's hand helps to convey the brief pain.

75

Here, one can permit the page to recede in focus. The need is to give each panel individual attention.

Isolating the sky-map makes it useable as a panel which adds time to the sequence.

Only the last scene employs the page as a superpanel

This page continues to serve as a single-sequence container, thereby becoming a unit. In effect it is a meta-panel — part of the whole chapter.

Another example of a flow of action gathered
and held by the open panel below.

78

This last page I designed to be swallowed whole. That is, I hoped the reader would see and feel the entire page as a panel. Then, steeped in the mood or message, read the newspapers which give the action depth.

THE SUPER-PANEL AS A PAGE

Where the super-panel purports to be a page—that is, to make the reader conscious of it as a page — it serves as a containment without perimeter. It is best employed for parallel narratives.

This narrative form, or device, has interesting potential not often explored in comics. The printed form lends itself to this because, unlike the transitory nature of the film medium, it can be referred to repeatedly throughout the reading. Obviously, it depends on the plot and careful planning.

In a plot where two independent narratives are shown simultaneously, the problem of giving them equal attention and weight is addressed by making the panel that controls the total narrative the entire page itself. The result, a set of panels within panels, attempts to control the reader's line of reading so that two storylines may be followed synchronously.

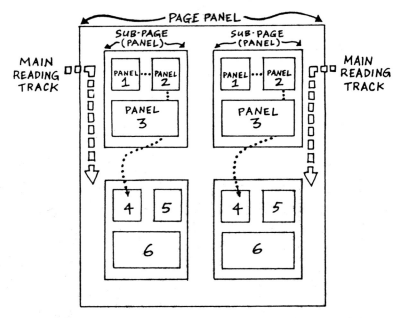

This diagram shows the reading track in such a device. Control of the reader's eye must be carefully considered.

In the following example from the *Spirit* story "TWO LIVES" (first published December 12, 1948), parallel development is both the solution of the problem of simultaneity and the actual theme of the plot itself.

In this story the perimeters of the total page — or any consciousness of it disappear after first perusal.

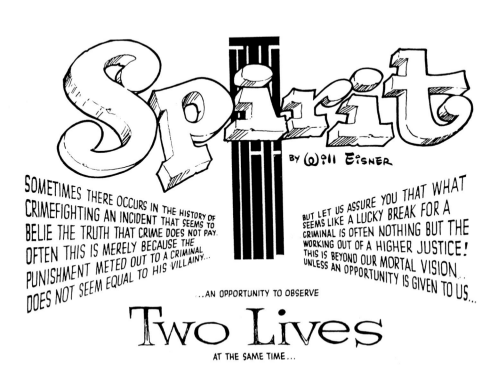

SOMETIMES THERE OCCURS IN THE HISTORY OF CRIMEFIGHTING AN INCIDENT THAT SEEMS TO BELIE THE TRUTH THAT CRIME DOES NOT PAY. OFTEN THIS IS MERELY BECAUSE THE PUNISHMENT METED OUT TO A CRIMINAL DOES NOT SEEM EQUAL TO HIS VILLAINY...

BUT LET US ASSURE YOU THAT WHAT SEEMS LIKE A LUCKY BREAK FOR A CRIMINAL IS OFTEN NOTHING BUT THE WORKING OUT OF A HIGHER JUSTICE! THIS IS BEYOND OUR MORTAL VISION... UNLESS AN OPPORTUNITY IS GIVEN TO US...

...AN OPPORTUNITY TO OBSERVE

Two Lives

AT THE SAME TIME...

...e reading track begins in the traditional manner. Each book is a visual device and a meta-...nel at the ...ame time.

The main reading track is vertical, but within each meta-panel it is traditional.

After the left hand side of the page is read, then the right hand column is read.

I designed the outline of each major panel as a book page, to insure against confusion.

In order to resume the "reality" of the page, I inserted 'false' panels under parallel pages. This device was intended to control the frame of reference.

83

Here, the resumption of the normal single page layout
returns the focus to the present tense.

The story now flows as a single narrative
with the action undivided.

85

By now the reader is moving along in
an atmosphere of normal situation.

86

This tier of panels acts as a bridge
bringing the reader to a 'surprise' ending.

°°° **A**ND SO...AS WE SAID...
. WHO AMONG US CAN ACCURATELY SAY WHAT IS A FIT PUNISHMENT ??
OR...IN THE WORDS OF HIS IMPERIAL MAJESTY, GILBERT & SULLIVAN'S EARNEST MIKADO OF JAPAN...

♫ *My object all sublime*
I shall achieve in time
To let the punishment fit the crime
The punishment fit the crime...♫

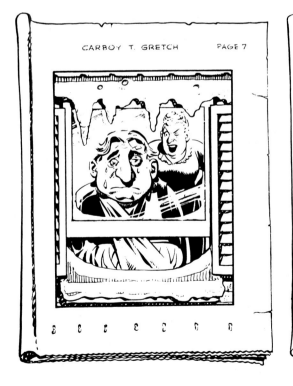

The parallel
narrative is
restored.

PANEL COMPOSITION

The composition of a comic strip panel is comparable to the planning of a mural, book illustration, easel painting or theatrical scene.

Once the flow of action is 'framed' it becomes necessary to compose the panel. This involves perspective and the arrangement of all the elements. The prime considerations are serving the flow of narrative and following standard reading conventions. Concern with mood, emotion, action and timing follows. Decoration or novelty of arrangement come into play only after these are resolved.

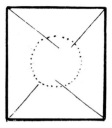   

1. A center of interest is established.

2. This becomes the site of the major action.

3. The perspective is now determined. (Note: the center of interest is not altered.)

4. The secondary narrative elements are added.

Functioning as a stage, the panel controls the viewpoint of the reader; the panel's outline becomes the perimeter of the reader's vision and establishes the perspective from which the site of the action is viewed. This manipulation enables the artist to clarify activity, orient the reader and stimulate emotion.

The reader's 'position' is assumed or predetermined by the artist. In each case the result is the view as the reader will see it.

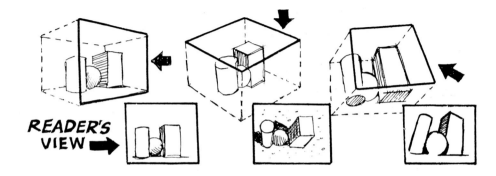

THE FUNCTION OF PERSPECTIVE

The primary function of perspective should be to manipulate the reader's orientation for a purpose in accord with the author's narrative plan. For example, accurate perspective is most useful when the sense of the story requires that the reader know precisely where all the elements of a drama are in relation to each other.

In this panel a flat eye-level view informs the reader of details such as the commanding action of the soldier's hand.	In this panel an over-head view is necessary to give the reader a clear uninvolved view of the setting and the events to follow.	In this panel the reader is placed on ground level to involve him so that the impact of the explosion can be 'felt.'	In this view the reader's perspective is lowered to a worm's eye-view for involvement in the action.

Another use of perspective is its employment to manipulate and produce various emotional states in the reader. I proceed from the theory that the viewer's response to a given scene is influenced by his positon as a spectator. Looking at a scene from above it the viewer has a sense of detachment — an observer rather than a participant. However, when the reader views a scene from below it, then his position evokes a sense of smallness which stimulates a sensation of fear. The shape of the panel in combination with perspective promotes these reactions because we are responsive to environment. A narrow panel evokes the feeling of being hemmed in — confinement, whereas a wide panel suggests plenty of space in which to move — or escape. These are deep seated primitive feelings and work when used properly.

The shape of the panel and the use of perspective within it can be manipulated to produce various emotional states in the viewer.

Panel A

In this example the oblong shape of the panel combined with the 'worm's eye' view from below evokes a sense of threat. The reader feels confined and dominated by the monster.

The same scene but viewed from 'a bird's eye' view from above and set in a wide panel stimulates the sense of detachment. The reader has plenty of elbow room and above it all. There is little threat or involvement.

Panel B.

90

REALISM AND PERSPECTIVE

In the main comics are a representational art form devoted to the emulation of real experience. The author/artist, therefore, in the pursuit of reality must be constantly concerned with perspective. Often he is confronted with a choice between the 'design' or 'impact' effect of the page and art versus the needs of the story. I regard this as an inherent problem because the primary task of the comic magazine publisher is to issue a 'package' that will be compelling at first glance to the buyer in the bookstore. As a result the integrity of the story telling is compromised. Indeed, the artist himself, becomes party to this subordination because the *first judgment* rendered onto any comic book work is centered on the art work; style, quality and draftsmanship. It is, after all, a graphic medium. In a field where the writer and the artist are two individuals whose professional reputation and earning power are dependent on recognition by the audience, the need for the artist to display artistic prowess even to the detriment of the story is quite irresistible. Often this results in an output of the story with virtuoso art work independent of — or even unrelated to the story. A representative example of a plot which needs careful discipline in art and perspective is the science fiction plot which tells of a supernatural occurrence in a realistic setting.

In the following *Spirit* story "THE VISITOR" (first published February 13, 1949) the requirements of stagecraft demand a firm head-on perspective throughout. This is for the purpose of increasing the sense of 'reality' in what would otherwise be a 'fantasy' plot.

However, in a plot of this kind the temptation to go 'hog-wild' with perspective shots and panel shapes is hard to resist. The carefully controlled and almost understated dissolve at the bottom of the last three panels on the story's last page is testimony to the discipline and restraint that is required to properly execute the surprise ending.

91

The graphic display on the splash page sets the mood. It creates a climate that promises a 'supernatural' or science-fiction theme.

All the scenes here are shown from an eye-level perspective to reinforce realism.

Here, the sole instance in which a birds-eye view is undertaken. The intention is an orientation for a 'normal,' every-day, believable setting.

Every effort is made to keep it believable. The babies crawling over the hero, the steady flat 'beat' of even ordinary (conventional) panels — all deliberately restrained

Even in the face of a provocative opportunity such as an astronomy laboratory, the eye-level discipline is rigidly maintained.

95

The profession of closeups here is a deliberate stratagem to lead the reader into an emotionally charged panel.

96

By now the reader's involvement is predicated on a sense of normalcy fostered by the unrelenting use of a flat-on perspective.

So, in the final resolution, where the sense of realism so critical to the surprise ending, the perspective that was used throughout the story is rigidly maintained.

98

A simple example of 'overkill' in layout and perspective is shown in the two alternate treatments shown below. Either of these are valid renderings of the action . . . if taken out of context. But, when examined in the light of their service to the story they are not useful.

Read the story as it was originally presented and then compare the alternate treatment given for the last two tiers on the last page. Below, a varied perspective is used as an end in itself — more for the sake of 'picture-interest' than storytelling. These two goals in comics are not always compatible, and one must weigh which is primary at any juncture: visual impact or narrative demands of the story.

Alternate Ending (A) The *'forced'* bird's eye perspective removes the reader from direct intimate involvement. This distraction interrupts his sense of normalcy.

Alternate Ending (B) The reader's position is made even more remote. Furthermore, removing the protagonist from close-up and suddenly allowing him to 'burst' from the panel concentrates everything on the act of flying. Flying, in this tier, is not as important as surprising the reader.

CHAPTER 5

EXPRESSIVE ANATOMY

By far the most universal image with which the sequential artist must deal is the human form. Of all the innumerable inventory of images that fill the human experience, the human form is the one most assiduously studied, and hence the most familiar.

The human body, and the stylization of its shape, and the codifying of its emotionally produced gestures and expressive postures are accumulated and stored in the memory, forming a non-verbal vocabulary of gesture. Unlike the frame device in comics, the postures of humans are not part of comic strip technology. They are rather a record " . . . of purposeful movement . . . a motor discharge . . . that can be a carrier of the expressive process."[1] They are part of the inventory of what the artist has retained from observation.

Not much is known about where or how the brain stores the countless bits of memory that contribute to or become comprehensible when arranged in a certain combination. But it is patently clear that when a skillfully limned image is presented it can trigger a recall that evokes recognition and the collateral effects on the emotion. We are obviously dealing here with the common memory of experience.

It is precisely because of this that the human form and the language of its bodily movements become one of the essential ingredients of comic strip art. The skill with which they are employed is also a measure of the author's ability to convey his idea.

[1]Hans Prinzhorn, "Artistry of the Mentally Ill," a contribution to the psychology and psychopathology of configuration. (Springer Verlag, 1972).

100

The relentless growth of communications technology since the dawn of man's intellectual history has served to universalize images of common human experience. Their employment in repetitive glyphs (later distilled into letters for language) makes them a code allowing memorization and deciphering. Perhaps the most obvious demonstration of this is in Egyptian hieroglyphics.

Early cave drawings are an example of written communication using familiar images.

Later, Egyptian friezes developed this further.

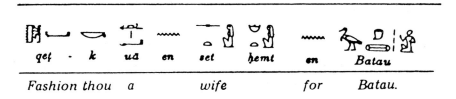

qet - k ua en set hemt en Batau

Fashion thou a wife for Batau.

Finally, the Egyptian Hieroglyphics codified the images into repeatable symbols to form a useable written language.

There have been many attempts to codify human postures and the emotions they register or reflect. In a popular modern book this was referred to as 'body language,' and a wide range of body posturing was assembled and defined. The fact is, however, that the 'reading' of human posture or gesture is an acquired skill which most humans possess to a greater degree than they know. Because it has to do with survival, humans begin to learn it from infancy. From postures we are warned of danger or told of love.

In comic book art, the artist must draw upon personal observations and an inventory of gestures, common and comprehensible to the reader. In effect, the artist must work from a 'dictionary' of human gestures.

101

A micro-DICTIONARY of GESTURES

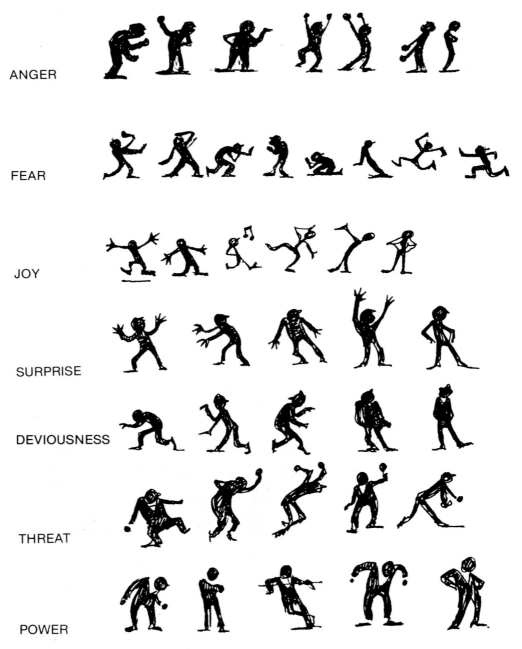

ANGER

FEAR

JOY

SURPRISE

DEVIOUSNESS

THREAT

POWER

These very simple abstractions of gestures and postures deal with external evidence of internal feelings. They serve to demonstrate, also, the enormous bank of symbols we build up out of our experience.

It is, I believe, appropriate at this point to defend the 'vanity' of trying (like daVinci) to make a science of art. Formal or organized recorded human communication began as visual communication. It is therefore not surprising that the artist can count on wide reader "reception" when a common gesture is limned so that it is easily recognized. The skill (and science if you will) lies in the selection of the posture or gesture. In the print medium, unlike film or theater, the practitioner has to distill a hundred intermediate movements of which the gesture is comprised into one posture. This selected posture must convey nuances, support the dialogue, carry the thrust of the story, and deliver the message.

THE BODY

In comics, body posture and gesture occupy a position of primacy over text. The manner in which these images are employed modifies and defines the intended meaning of the words. They can by their relevance to the reader's own experience invoke a nuance of emotion and give auditory inflection to the voice of the speaker.

103

If the skill with which an actor emulates an emotion is, in large part, the criterion for evaluating his or her ability, certainly the artist's performance at delineating the same on paper must be measured with the same yardstick. In comic strip art this property is widely employed.

It would take a book in itself to catalogue the thousands of gestures and postures with which humans communicate visually. For the purpose of this discussion, it is necessary only to examine and demonstrate the relationship of gesture or posture to dialogue and to observe the result of its application.

A GESTURE, generally almost idiomatic to a region or culture, tends to be subtle and limited to a narrow range of movement. Usually, it is the final position that is the key to its meaning. The selection process here is confined to the context within a sequence. It must clearly convey intended meaning. The reader must agree with the selection. The reader decides whether the choice is appropriate.

In this example there are a few instantly recognizable gestures. Of the thousands of possible gestures that accompany human postures or attitudes a surprising number are universal.

104

A POSTURE is a movement selected out of a sequence of related moments in a single action. In the example that follows, one posture must be selected out of a flow of movements in order to tell a segment of a story. It is then frozen into the panel in a block of time.

These examples summarize a series of very subtle movements which take place in a very *short* period of time—but which are meant to imply a '*held*' motion in the flow of narrative.

In a panel selected from a series, the frozen posture tells its story—giving information about the before and after of the event.

This event takes place over a *short* period of time — but because there was a need to clearly show the source of the weapon (rock) and the power needed to effectively use it — the action was broken up into three panels.

In this example, a whole sequence of postures that immediately precede the one shown is assumed. It is acceptable simply because the moment of time frozen in this action sums it up with the understanding that the viewer knows (and can supply imaginatively) that there could not have been any other set of postures possible in order to arrive at this point. The postures that follow immediately are also assumed and it is unnecessary to depict them unless the next panel depends on the outcome of the movement.

Out of a series of 8 motions that comprise an action of about 30-seconds duration, one representative post is 'frozen.' It is selected after considering its relationship to preceeding and succeeding panels.

ALTERNATE SELECTION OF POSTURE

If, for example the narrative requires that the final thrust of the warrior's shield is the main point in this segment of narrative then the posture selected is the final movement in this 30-second motion.

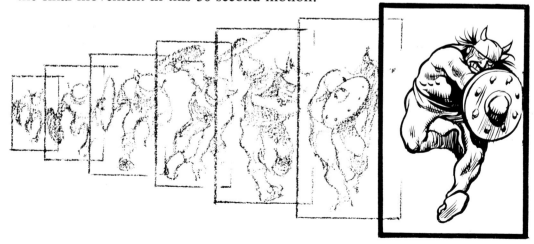

This three frame sequence is taken out of a series of movements that takes place over a period of perhaps one hour or more. The selection, or 'freezing,' of key postures seeks to communicate time as well as emotion. Each posture is of equal importance in the narrative.

INTERMEDIATE ACTION

The in-between actions are implied by each pose shown.

Out of these, the reader can deduce the choreography.

NOTHIN'...JUST A MIRAGE...

The following page demonstrates a more complex application and deployment of postures and gestures selected out of intermediate actions. Here is an effort to give the reader much more of an insight into a character's life-style — to make a sociological observation.

From Will Eisner's "THE BIG CITY" first published in the SPIRIT Magazine #35, June 1982.

THE FACE

In most conventional books on human anatomy it is customary to treat the head as an appendage. In comic book art this part of the anatomy invites the most attention and involvement. For the sake of this discussion, the face is studied without regard to individual personality.

The following example demonstrates the response of muscular reflex (contortion) in the face that reflects or gives evidence of an inner emotion.

Pain . . . a painful effort . . .
a pain in some part of the body.

Discomfort in some part of
the body . . . perhaps internal.

Comfort that extends over
the entire body. Pleasure.

Body is poised for some
movement, flight or action.

The distinction between posture and gesture in the face is less definable because of the limits of its anatomy. Except for the ears and nose the surface of the face is in constant motion. Eyebrows, lips, jaws, eyelids and cheeks are responding to muscular movements triggered by an emotional switchboard in the brain.

Here is a demonstration of the effect of a commonly understood set of facial postures (grimaces??) which give meaning to a parallel set of statements. The intention is to display the application of facial expressions as a vocabulary.

The surface of the face is, as someone once put it, "a window to the mind." It is familiar terrain to most humans. Its role in communication is to register emotion. On this surface the combinations of the moveable elements are expected by the reader to reveal an emotion and act as an adverb to the posture or gesture of the body. Because of this relationship, the head (or face) is often used by artists to convey the entire message of bodily movement. It is the one part of the body with which the reader is most familiar. The face also, of course, provides meaning to the spoken word. Unlike the body, its gestures are more subtle but more readily understood. It is also the part of the body that is most individual. From the reading of a face, people make daily judgments, entrust their money, political future and their emotional relationships. I have often mused that if animals' faces were more flexible, more individual, more reflective of emotions, they might be less easily killed by humans.

This simply illustrates the adverbial effect of the posture of the head on the movement of features on the surface of the face. Together they communicate the emotional reaction to an unheard (by the reader) telephone message.

THE BODY AND THE FACE

The employment of body posture and facial expression (both having equal attention) is a major undertaking and an area of frequent failure. Properly and skillfully done, it can carry the narrative without resorting to unnecessary props or scenery. The use of expressive anatomy in the absence of words is less demanding because the latitude for the art is wider. Where the words have a depth of meaning and nuance, the task is more difficult.

The following example "Hamlet On A Rooftop" (first published in June 1981) attempts to address such a challenge.

111

This represents an example of a classic situation — that of author vs. artist. The artist must decide at the outset what his 'input' shall be; to slavishly make visual that which is in the author's mind or to embark on the raft of the author's words onto a visual sea of his own charting.

HAMLET ON A ROOFTOP

His father is dead, mysteriously! His mother, within but a month, marries his uncle! So soon?, so soon? Can there be anything other than **something rotten** here? Can it be anything but murder!? Well, then, if murder it be all he values, indeed, his manhood cries out for retribution ....vengeance .. to honor the filial duty his father's voice demands in the hot cauldron of his mind! Aye, to punish them, to **murder his mother and uncle**... as they lay in violation of his code!!! ...or perhaps something more unspeakable within him.

Yet... can he find in himself the capacity to commit so unnatural an act and in doing it forfeit the love of Ophelia, his betrothed? Wait... hold still for a moment, cling briefly to a passing raft of reason before it leaves the brain, before surrendering to the swift river of his passion, and so to be carried out into the turgid sea of violence from which there is no return.

46

In this experiment, Shakespeare's words are intact. The soliloquy is broken up into balloons at the artist's discretion. The intent here is to permit a meaningful fusing of word, imagery and timing. The result should provide the reader with necessary pauses.

The artist here functions as actor and in the process gives his own meaning to the lines.

A gesture signifying contemplation.

Furniture employed in intimate involvement with the actor gives the 'background' story value because it is part of the action.

Submission . . . to a "heavy" thought.

Here, the postures are more than a classical portrayal of emotions. This man is not the Danish Prince Hamlet! His gestures and postures are derivative of his special background. The question of how he would deliver the standard gesture for self-doubt and internal agony is the artist's real challenge!

WHETHER 'TIS NOBLER IN THE MIND TO SUFFER THE SLINGS AND ARROWS OF OUTRAGEOUS FORTUNE...

OR...

TO TAKE ARMS AGAINST A SEA OF TROUBLES, AND BY OPPOSING **END** THEM!

Bravado . . . he envisions himself as challenging the forces of troubles

114

Exhaustion — beaten by the enormity of his problems

Seeking comfort he lets his body slide down along the wall

Retreat . . . into his refuge . . . sleep

The language of posture is universal and inter-changeable — the application is not.

Wishing with all his might.

Withdraw-ing into sleep or oblivion, he assumes an almost fetal posture.

Awake again to the thoughts that will not leave him!

Candor . . addressing the unseen manipulator of his fate

116

Arguing
. . . he
begins to
make a
~~e to but-~~
~~ss grow-~~
resolve.

117

6.

The use of a
ng-shot, here
is meant to
reinforce
alism — and
that way try
deal with the
problem of
putting
nakespeare's
guage in the
outh of such
a man.

sitation . . .
a recurrence
of doubt

RESOLVE!

This wedding of Shakespearean language with a modern denizen of the ghetto may not be appropriate but the exercise serves to demonstrate the potential of the medium because the emotional content is so universal.

CHAPTER 6

WRITING &
SEQUENTIAL ART

'Writing' for comics can be defined as the conception of an idea, the arrangement of image elements and the construction of the sequence of the narration and the composing of dialogue. It is at once a part and the whole of the medium. It is a special skill, its requirements not always in common with other forms of 'writing' for it deals with a singular technology. It is closest in requirements to playwriting, but for the fact that the writer, in the case of comics, is also the imagemaker (artist).

In sequential art the two functions are irrevocably interwoven. Sequential art is the act of weaving a fabric.

In writing with words alone, the author directs the reader's imagination. In comics the imagining is done for the reader. An image once drawn becomes a precise statement that brooks little or no further interpretation. When the two are "mixed" the words become welded to the image and no longer serve to describe but rather to provide sound, dialogue and connective passages.

THE WRITER AND THE ARTIST

In order to consider, separately, the role of the writer, it is necessary to arbitrarily limit the 'writing' for comics to the function of conceiving the idea and the story, creating the order of telling and fabricating the dialogue or narrative elements. With this as a given, we can arrange an order of progression which assembles itself as follows:

The idea and the story or plot in the form of a written script includes narrative and dialogue (balloons).

The deployment of words and the architecture of the structure composed expands or develops the concept of the story. Directions to the artist (description of panel and page content) carry that idea from the mind of the writer to the illustrator.

Each component pledges allegiance to the whole. The writer must at the outset be concerned with the interpretation of his story by the artist, and the artist must allow himself to be a captive of the story or idea. The separate considerations of the writing and drawing functions are directly involved with the aesthetics of the medium because the actual segregation of the writing and art function has proliferated in the practice of modern comics.

Unlike theatre (including cinema), in which the technology of its creation demands by its very nature the coordinated contributions of many specialists, comics have a history of being the product of a single individual.

The departure from the work of a single individual to that of a team is generally due to the exigency of time. More often the publisher ordains it out of a need to meet publication schedules, control his property when he owns a character, or when his editor assembles a team to suit an editorial thrust.

Many times the artist will bow to the editor's opinion that he has limited 'writing' skills—or the artist will voluntarily abdicate the 'writing' role. So, to accommodate the dictates of the publisher or schedule, the artist will engage the services of a writer, or the writer will engage the skills of an artist. A bemusing result of this phenomenon has been the dilemma faced by modern comic book publishers when they have sought to return to the creator the 'originals' after publication. Who is the 'creator' of a comic page which was written by one person, penciled by another and inked, lettered (and perhaps colored or backgrounded) by still others??

A factor that has always had an impact on comics as an art form is the underlying reality that we are dealing with a medium of expression which is primarily visual. Artwork dominates the reader's initial attention. This then lures the artist to concentrate his skills on style, technique and graphic devices which are designed to dazzle the eye. The reader's receptivity to the sensory effect and often his evaluation of its worth reinforces this concern and encourages the proliferation of artistic athletes who produce pages of absolutely stunning art held together by almost no story at all.

123

THE APPLICATION OF "WRITING"

In comics that serve an essentially visually oriented audience or where the story demands are oriented toward a simple superhero, the action and style of art becomes so dominant that it mitigates the 'weave' of writing and art. Another factor in the loosening of this fabric is the procedure whereby the writer gives the artist the bare summary of a plot. The artist proceeds to create an entire sequence of art, composing his panels around a general assumption of unwritten dialogue and the satisfaction of his perception of the plot's requirements. The completed work (at this point little more than a tapestry) is returned to the writer who must then apply dialogue and connecting narrative. Under these circumstances there could occur a struggle for identity as the writer, seeking to maintain his equity in the end product, overwrites in spaces arbitrarily allocated to him by the artist who has created an interpretation that is now irrevocable.

WORDS/ART: INSEPARABLE

The following simple example of the interdependency of words (text) and image (art) undertakes a theme of some sophistication. In this case the art without the text would be quite meaningless. Here the artist is also 'writing.'

The positioning of the fish and the unembellished rendering of the art does not intrude on the theme. The deliberate pause (timing) by the insertion of a wordless panel adds weight and power to the punch line. Making the words BELIEVE, GOD and WHO boldface adds sound and disciplines the reader's internal ear. In reality, the reader is being asked to supply (or 'hear') the sound internally.

This is an aspect of 'writing' especially adaptable to comics. The 'control' of the *reader's ear* is vital if the meaning and intent of the dialogue is to remain as the writer intended it.

THE APPLICATION OF WORDS

Assume for this example a script (segment) prepared by either the writer or the artist which deals with a fugitive who is running away from pursuing police. Here we seek a demonstration of the various possible applications of text which include dialogue, connecting narrative and description. Remember that in creativity there is no 'right' or 'wrong.'

EXAMPLE 1 (Humor): A 'pure' visual! The 'writing,' which may either have preceded the creation of the art in the form of a couple of sentences of description or been described orally, is dispensed with entirely.

EXAMPLE 2 (Humor): Since humor deals in exaggerated simplification, so must the "writing." Because of the simplicity of the art, text can (and has the freedom to) alter either meaning or intent. It can also affect the humor by adding a dimension of incongruity.

125

EXAMPLE 3 (realism): A minimum of word usage. Words here are employed for sounds. The artist shoulders the burden of conveying the action and the emotion of the fugitive by imagery alone.

EXAMPLE 4 (realism): Balloons are more liberally used to reinforce the theme.

EXAMPLE 5 (realism): A heavy application of narrative seeks to add dimension to the art and tries to participate in the story-telling by repeating (or reinforcing) what the images are trying to tell.

126

In view of this interdependence there is therefore no choice (in fairness to the art form itself) but to recognize the primacy of the writing. In doing so, however, one must then immediately acknowledge that in a perfect (or pure) configuration the writer and the artist should be embodied in the same person. The writing (or the writer) must be in control to the very end.

STORY AND IMAGERY

In practice the creator, given or having conceived the idea, sets about to develop it with words and imagery into a unified whole. It is here that the graphic elements ascend to dominance. For the end product is, after all, to be read as a total visual. It is this 'mix' which is, in the final analysis, the ultimate test of the success and quality of the sequential art effort.

STORY DEVELOPMENT

From the outset the conception and writing of a story is affected by the limitations of the medium. These virtually dictate the scope of a story and the depth of its telling. It is for this reason that stories and plots of simple, obvious action have long dominated comic book literature. The selection of a story and the telling of it, become subject to limitations of space, skill of the artist and the technology of reproduction. Actually, from the viewpoint of art or literature, this medium can deal with subject matter and theme of great sophistication.

Of the many elements of a story the most amenable to imagery are scenery and action. It is also reasonable to expect this medium to deal with abstractions that can be conveyed by human action and scenery. The dialogue which gives voice to the thought processes has the effect of rendering action meaningful. Text used in the introduction of a sequence or interposed between panels is employed to deal with the passage of time and changes in locale. In this connection, perhaps the most useful (and most used) word in comics is "MEANWHILE."

There is no absolute ratio of words-to-picture in a medium where words (lettering) are in themselves part of the form. Sequential art operates under a rule of thumb that defines an image as either a 'visual' or an ' illustration.' I define a 'visual' as a series or sequence of images that replace a descriptive passage told only in words. An 'illustration' reinforces (or decorates) a descriptive passage. It simply *repeats* the text.

It is the 'VISUAL' that functions as the purest form of sequential art because it seeks to employ a mix of letters and images as a language in dealing with narration.

At the outset the creator makes a determination as to the nature of the story. He must determine if he is dealing with the exposition of an idea, a problem and its solution or the conveyance of the reader through an experience.

The style of treatment (i.e. humorous or realistic) has an obvious importance in the considerations that follow. Most often this is a predetermined concept and is eliminated from conscious choice or protracted deliberation. It is nonetheless important to factor it in the following steps.

In the next step the story is "broken down." At this time the application of the story and plot to the limitations of space or technology of the conveyance takes place. Page size, number of pages, reproduction process and available colors influence the "breakdown." Sometimes, particularly in the situation where the script is prepared by a writer for an artist, the fundamental breakdown is performed by the writer in the process of his work. The writer initiates the breakdown and expects (very often with a fervent prayer) the artist to reproduce or convert into visuals the description of action and compositional instructions that accompany the dialogue. Obviously, a close rapport between the two will prevent impossible demands by the writer and confounding modifications (generally in the form of abbreviations and downright omissions) by the artist who is often struggling more with the limitations of space, time and skill of rendering (not to mention laziness) than with intellectual considerations.

It takes a very sophisticated writer of long experience and dedication to accept total castration of his words, as, for example, a series of exquisitely written balloons which are discarded in favor of an equally exquisite pantomine. Where the artist must deal with or is forced to preserve the inviolability of the writer's words (as in dialogue or narrative passages) the result is often a string of 'talking heads.' Where the writer is capable of accompanying his text with sketches as an integral part of the script the problem is less severe.

128

Of course, where the writer and the artist are the same person these problems are somewhat buried in the thinking process of the writer/artist and are laundered in the flow of decision making. But he must, nevertheless, go through the entire process whether or not he does it on a set of thumbnails (writing dialogue as he goes) or follows the formality of typing a script for his own use. Here, at least, the writer's sovereignty and equity are no longer involved.

This is a simplified example of an average script. In practice the presentation style of the script varies with the standards of the publishing house — or the agreement between artist and writer. This script deals with only one page of a story.

```
                        Page 2

PANEL 1

        NARRATIVE:   Meanwhile...

          SPIRIT:   "Look here, Dolan, the city
                     is crawling with
                     GRANCH's hoods.  You've
                     got to do something."

           DOLAN:   "What?  They've done
                     nothing!"

           SCENE:    In Dolan's office it's
                     night time after hours.
                     The only light is from
                     Dolan's desk lamp.
                     The Spirit is looking
                     out the window - out
                     to the city.  It is a
                     big city police com-
                     missioner's office.

PANEL 2

          SPIRIT:   "yet!!"

           SCENE:    The Spirit, pensive,
                     still looking out the
                     window.
```

PANEL 3

      DOLAN: "Unless..someone...
                  on the side of the
                  law, of course...were
                  to...!"

      SCENE: Dolan's getting a
                  brainstorm. His face
                  shows a crafty idea
                  is aborning. Per-
                  haps a close up, his
                  face lit by the lone
                  lamp.

PANEL 4

      NARRATIVE: Two hours later....

      SCENE: The waterfront of
                  Central City. Fog
                  swirls about the
                  piles and rotting
                  planking of the
                  wharf. We see the
                  Spirit standing in
                  the one spot of
                  light provided by
                  a lone lamp post.
                  The hull of a docked
                  tanker is barely
                  visible in the mist.
                  In a corner of the
                  panel we see a
                  shadowy figure — —
                  obviously a thug.

PANEL 5

      THUG: "Welcome to our
                  turf...don't move
                  a muscle!!"

      SPIRIT: "Well, well...
                  GRANCH's hos-
                  pitality corps
                  ...tch, tch!!"

      SCENE: Close in on the Spirit
                  ...Out of the shadows
                  the thug moves close
                  to the Spirit..We see
                  his glistening knife
                  blade pointed to just
                  behind the Spirit's
                  ear. The thug is
                  dimly seen. The
                  Spirit's posture is
                  one of seeming sur-
                  render.

This flow chart shows the thinking process and the steps of development from the script of a single page (shown in detail on the preceding pages) to the pencil stage ready for finished (inking) art.

I have always been strongly of the opinion that the writer and artist should be in one person. Failing that, and in the absence of any prior agreement between artist and writer, then I come down in favor of the dominance of the artist. This is not to free him from the obligation to work in service of the story originated by the writer. Rather, I expect him to shoulder this burden with the understanding that with the so called 'freedom' will come a greater challenge — that of employing or devising a wider range of visual devices and composition innovation. He should contribute to the 'writing.'

In any event, in any ideal scriptwriter-artist relationship the artist must assume the burden of two major freedoms, omission and addition. For those who would like to have a rule these two might be useful.

OMISSION OF TEXT

The artist should be free to omit dialogue or narrative that can clearly be demonstrated visually.

AS DIRECTED BY SCRIPT   AS ARTIST MODIFIES IT

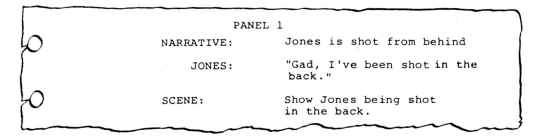

```
                        PANEL 1
          NARRATIVE:        Jones is shot from behind

             JONES:        "Gad, I've been shot in the
                           back."

             SCENE:        Show Jones being shot
                           in the back.
```

132

ADDITION OF TEXT/ART

The artist should be free to enlarge a sequence of panels to create 'timing' which reinforces the intent of the script.

THE SCRIPT AS THE WRITER PRODUCED IT. Actually, the writer will generally concentrate on plot and dialogue leaving (or hoping) for skillful stage craft by the artist. Shown here is a two panel segment of script.

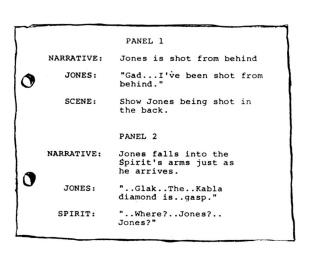

```
                              PANEL 1

              NARRATIVE:    Jones is shot from behind

                 JONES:    "Gad...I've been shot from
                           behind."

                 SCENE:    Show Jones being shot in
                           the back.


                              PANEL 2

              NARRATIVE:    Jones falls into the
                           Spirit's arms just as
                           he arrives.

                 JONES:    "..Glak..The..Kabla
                           diamond is..gasp."

                SPIRIT:    "..Where?..Jones?..
                           Jones?"
```

The artist has *added* two panels to create a 'timing' element that increases the drama. By splitting the dying man's dialogue the man's demise is visualized. Furthermore, the elimination of narrative makes the reading flow uninterrupted. This is story-telling by the artist.

133

This story was written by Jules Feiffer for a 4 page SPIRIT story to have been run October 12, 1952. It was never executed or published.

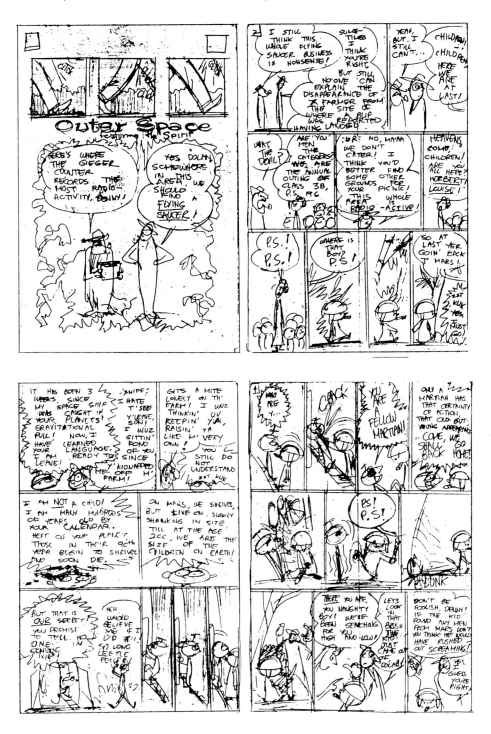

This is an example of a 'script' produced by a writer who is also skilled at drawing.

Since he can sketch he is able to supply the artist with visual stage directions.

But an even more important ingredient is the writer's understanding of the artist's style and capabilities. The compatability of the writer and artist is very evident here.

An example of a typical script style. This allows the artist to innovate page layouts and panel composition.

Page 1 [missing]

Page 2

Panel 1 -- (Martian) zzzt.. clk.. RUINED!

Panel 2 -- (Martian) MY BEAUTIFUL SPACESHIP DESTROYED BY THAT LITTLE BEAST WITH A PEPPERMINT STICK! HOW CAN I EVER REPAIR IT WITHOUT NEW PARTS?

Panel 3 -- (Martian) HOW CAN I EVER RETURN TO MARS? I AM DOOMED, DOOMED TO REMAIN ON EARTH! [Martian turns on television]

Panel 4 -- (Television Announcer) AND IN TONIGHT'S DEBATE, THE SPIRIT ANNOUNCED HE WILL PROVE THE POSSIBILITY OF FLYING SAUCERS BY REVEALING A FOUR FOOT REPLICA OF A SAUCER COMPLETE WITH ALL PARTS!

Panel 5 -- (Television Announcer) DESIGNED BY LEADING SCIENTISTS AND WORKABLE, THIS SAUCE... CLICK--- (Martian) HA!

Panel 6 -- (Martian) I HAVE FOUND A WAY TO RETURN TO MARS!

Panel 7 -- Caption: THAT NIGHT... (Skeptical Scientist, in a television studio) ACCORDING TO PUBLIC RELEASES, A FLYING SAUCER WILL BE REVEALED HERE TONIGHT! I CAN ONLY SCOFF AT THIS! FLYING SAUCERS DO NOT EXIST!

Page 3

Panel 1 -- (Skeptical Scientist) THEY ARE MERE ILLUSIONS OF LIGHT. NOTHING THE SPIRIT CAN SAY, NO SO-CALLED SAUCER WHICH HE CAN REVEAL, WILL PROVE OTHERWISE! (Dolan, sitting on a stage with The Spirit) DO YOU REALLY HAVE A SAUCER? (Spirit, also on stage) SHH... YES. IT'S IN THE BACK ROOM!

Panel 2 -- Caption: IN THE BACK ROOM... [Martian sneaking into back room through open door]

Panel 3 -- [Silent -- probably long view showing past Martian to group of kids outside back room door. P.S. Smith (whose actual name is Algernon Tidewater) can be seen with kids and parents or teacher. Dolan is approaching room too, from opposite direction.]

Panel 4 -- (Parent or Teacher) P.S., WHERE ARE YOU GOING? [P.S. is leaving group, heading for back room.]

Panel 5 -- (Parent or Teacher, off panel) P.S., COME ON BACK! (Martian) P.S.— THAT'S THE MONSTER WHO RUINED MY SHIP!

Panel 6 -- [Silent — P.S. enters back room and confronts Martian]

Panel 7 -- [Silent — P.S. probably knocks Martian out with his peppermint stick.]

Panel 8 -- (Dolan, just entering back room) P.S., DON'T GO IN THERE! [P.S. is entering saucer.]

Panel 9 -- [Saucer is taking off with P.S. in it] (Dolan, having entered now-empty back room) NOW, WHERE DID HE GO!

Page 4

Panel 1 -- (Skeptical Scientist in studio) IN CONCLUSION, I REPEAT, THESE SAUCERS DO NOT EXIST!

Panel 2 -- (Skeptical Scientist) THEY ARE ILLUSIONS! ...MERE... ILLUSIONS! [As he talks, we see behind him through window a view of the saucer flying by.]

Panel 3 -- (Television Announcer, gesturing toward The Spirit) AND NOW FOR REBUTTAL, I GIVE YOU THE SPIRIT!

Panel 4 -- (Spirit) MY ONLY REBUTTAL, GENTLEMEN, WILL BE AN ACTUAL DEMONSTRATION OF A FLYING SAUCER! COMMISSIONER DOLAN, BRING IN THE SAUCER!

Panel 5 -- (Spirit, impatiently) COMMISSIONER DOLAN...

Panel 6 -- (Spirit, very impatiently) WHAT DO YOU MEAN YOU CAN'T? IT'S IN THE BACK ROOM! (Dolan) THE BACK ROOM IS EMPTY!

Panel 7 -- (Jeering Audience) HA HA! HA HA! FAKE! HA HA HA HA HA!

Panel 8 -- Caption: LATER... [P.S. is back on Earth, holding some outlandish Martian artifact, still sucking his candy stick. Dolan absent-mindedly notices him but doesn't see the saucer behind them, or the Martian who is even now running eagerly toward it.] (Dolan) OH, THERE YOU ARE, P.S. WHERE'D YOU PICK UP THAT DUMB-LOOKING TOY!

Panel 9 -- Caption: MEANWHILE... [and we see that the poor battered Martian has finally made it back into outer space, as the saucer heads toward Mars.]

THE END

THE DUMMY

For the graphic medium the conceptual layout is an almost inescapable requirement. In advertising it is called a layout or mechanical, in film making it is the story boards and in comics it is a "dummy".

This device functions as a trial mock up which gives the creator the chance to make rearrangements before the final product is begun. In comics a dummy is an indispensable tool because successful graphic story telling depends on the ability of the text and imagery arrangement to convey the narrative and hold the reader's attention. This instrument provides the editor, writer and artist with control of story and art. The time and money saving advantages are obvious.

The following dummy shows several pages from a graphic novel TO THE HEART OF THE STORM. It was executed on 8 1/2" X 11" typewriter sheets, approximately the size and shape of the final printed page. The inked page is shown alongside.

136

This pencil dummy page is comprehensive enough for editor and artist.

The inking shows refinements in posture and layout. Working from a dummy the artist enjoys a great deal of freedom in that there is an underlying structure upon which the rendering can depend.

CHAPTER 7

APPLICATION
(The Use of Sequential Art)

In general terms we can divide the functions of Sequential Art into two broad applications; instruction and entertainment. Periodical comics, graphic novels, instructional manuals and storyboards are the most familiar vehicles. In the main, periodical comics and graphic novels are devoted to entertainment while manuals and storyboards are used to instruct or sell. But there is an overlap because art in sequence tends to be expository. For instance, comic books, which generally confine themselves to stories designed exclusively for entertainment, often employ instructional techniques which buttress the exaggeration and enhance the entertainment. In a work of comic art intended purely for entertainment, some technical exposition of a precise nature often occurs. A common example is a procedure like the opening of a safe in a detective story or the assembling of parts in a space adventure. This technical passage is actually a set of images with an instructional message embedded in an 'entertaining' story.

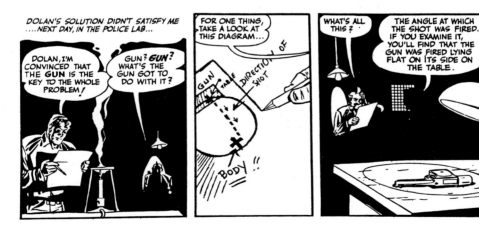

In this three panel sequence from the *Spirit* story "THE GUILTY GUN" (first published June 6, 1948), an 'entertainment' comic, the technical ballistics information needed for reader comprehension is imparted subtly enough that it does not detract from the forward motion of the plot.

139

In the case of a purely instructional comic, particularly in the case of a behavioral or attitudinal piece, the specifics of the information are frequently overlarded with humor (exaggeration) to attract the reader's attention, convey relevance, and set up visual analogies and recognizable life situations. This inserts 'entertainment' into a 'technical' work.

ENTERTAINMENT COMICS

Obviously sequential art is not without limitations. An image, wordlessly depicting a gesture or a scene, can, for example, convey depths and a certain amount of emotion. But as we observed earlier in the discussion on writing, images are specific, so they obviate interpretation. An assemblage of art that portrays life allows little input of an imaginative nature from the reader. However, the recognition by the reader of real-life people portrayed in the art and the addition of "in-between" action are supplied by the reader out of his own experiences. In the main, though, these requirements on the reader are set down with precision by the art.

There is a kind of privacy which the reader of a traditional prose work enjoys in the process of translating a descriptive passage into a visual image in the mind. This is a very personal thing and permits an involvement far more participatory than the voyeurism of examining a picture.

Another challenge to the sequential art medium is the matter of dealing with abstraction. Obviously, when the comic artist selects a single posture out of a chain of motions by a body—or an arrested moment in the animation of objects in movement—there is little time (or space) to deal with the amorphics of, say, the surge of pain or the glow of love or the turmoil of inner conflicts. When faced with this task, the demand on the innovativeness and creativity of the comic artist becomes enormous. Yet it is precisely in these areas where the opportunity for expansion of the application of comic book art lies. This is the prime and continuous confrontation which the comic book cartoonist must address. There are only two ways to deal with it: to try, and risk failure, or not to do it at all—that is, to avoid any subject not easily expressed by the present state of the art or its existing cliches.

THE GRAPHIC NOVEL

In recent years a new horizon has come into sharp focus with the emergence of the 'graphic novel,' a form of comic book that is still in fetal development. The efforts at this application of the medium, random and enthusiastic as they are, still run headlong into an unprepared audience, not to mention an ill-equipped distribution system that provides an adequate position in the general marketplace where display usually follows the patterns of yesterday.

Historically, comics have been confined to short narrations or depictions of episodes of brief but intense duration. Indeed, the reader, it was assumed, sought from comics either instant visually transmittable information, as in daily strips, or a visual experience of a sensory nature, as in the fantasy comics. Between 1940 and the early sixties the industry commonly accepted the profile of the comic book reader as that of a '10-year old from Iowa.' In adults the reading of comic books was regarded as a sign of low intelligence. Publishers neither encouraged nor supported anything more.

Early tapestries, friezes or hieroglyphic narrations either recorded events or sought to reinforce mythologies; they spoke to a broad audience. In the middle ages, when sequential art sought to tell morality tales or religious stories with no great depth of discussion or nuance, the readership addressed was one with little formal education. In this way, sequential art developed into a kind of shorthand which employed stereotypes when addressing human involvement. Those readers who sought greater sophistication of subject and greater subtlety and complexity of narrative could find it more easily by learning how to read words. Future application of sequential art will find this its major challenge.

The future for the graphic novel lies in the choice of worthwhile themes and the innovation of exposition. Given the fact that, despite the proliferation of electronic technology, the portable printed page will remain in place for the immediate future, it would seem that the attraction to it of a more sophisticated audience lies in the hands of serious comic book artists and writers who are willing to risk trial and error. Publishers are only catalysts. No more should be expected from them.

The future of this form awaits participants who truly believe that the application of sequential art, with its interweaving of words and pictures, could provide a dimension of communication that contributes—hopefully on a level never before attained—to the body of literature that concerns itself with the examination of human experience. The art then is that of deploying images and words, each in exquisitely balanced proportion, within the limitations of the medium and in the face of the still unresolved ambivalence of the audience toward it.

Style, presentation, the economy of space and the technological nature of reproduction notwithstanding, balloons and panels are still the basic tools with which to work. As for the receptivity of the audience, this must (and will) change and become sympathetic as the product delivers more and becomes more relevant.

TECHNICAL INSTRUCTION COMICS

In the arena of instructional visuals—or the application of sequential art to teach something specific—the limitations which afflict purely entertaining comics are less mitigating. There are two forms of instructional comics, 'technical' and 'attitudinal.'

This example of a *Joe Dope* story appeared in the first issue of P.S. Magazine the Preventive Maintenance Monthly published by the Department of Defence in 1951.

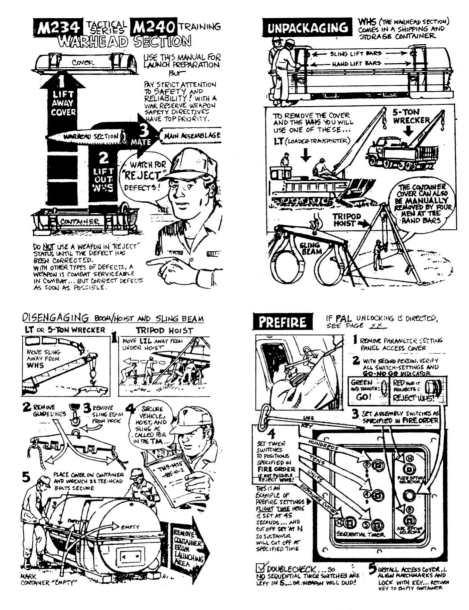

These are sample pages from an operator's manual used by the military. It shows a more formal layout that retains the function of panels and balloons.

A purely ' technical ' comic, in which the procedure to be learned is shown from the reader's point of view, gives instruction in procedures, process, and task performance generally associated with such things as assemblies of devices or their repair. The performance of such tasks are, in themselves, sequential in nature and the success of this art form as a teaching tool lies in the fact that the reader can easily relate to the experience demonstrated. For example, the most successful exposition of a procedure is one that is shown from the reader's perspective. Here the arrangement of panels, the position of the balloons and/or explanatory text carefully arranged on a page are all calculated to involve the reader. Properly done, these elements should combine to provide the reader with a familiarity born out of the experience that sequential art is so good at providing.

ATTITUDINAL INSTRUCTION COMICS

Another instructional function of this medium is conditioning an attitude toward a task. The relationship or the identification evoked by the acting out or dramatization in a sequence of pictures is in itself instructional. People learn by imitation and the reader in this instance can easily supply the intermediate or connecting action from his or her own experience. Here too there is no pressure of time as there would be in a live action motion picture or animated film. The amount of time allowed to the reader of a printed comic to examine, digest and imagine the process of acting out or assuming the role or attitude demonstrated is unlimited. There is room for approximation and opportunity for specific performances which the reader can examine without pressure. Unlike the rigidity of photographs, the broad generalization of artwork permits exaggeration which can more quickly make the point and influence the reader.

Designed for career exploration. (Grade 4 to 12) JOB SCENE booklets give students a sense of personal responsibility for their careers. They stress the potency and dignity of work, introduce a wide variety of job opportunities, stimulate interest and whet curiosity.

STORY BOARDS

Story Boards are 'still' scenes for motion pictures, pre-planned and laid-out in hand painted or drawn frames. While they employ the major elements of sequential art, they depart from comic books and strips in that they dispense with balloons and panels. They are not mean to be 'read' but rather to bridge the gap between the movie script and the final photography of the film. In practice the story board suggests "shots" (camera angles) and envisions the staging and lighting.

Because of the fundamental relationship between film and the comics which preceded it, there is little surprise in the fact that the employment of comic book artists by film makers has boomed.

Here is an example of a story board for a commercial and the resulting film shown below.

BOLLA BRUT, "Party F/P," The Joseph Garneau Company, Copyright 1984.

146

CHAPTER 8

TEACHING/LEARNING
Sequential Art for Comics
IN THE
PRINT AND COMPUTER ERA

Sequential art, especially as it is applied to comics is, in the main, intended for reproduction. Therefore, the aesthetics and technical skills must be addressed almost simultaneously. There is little opportunity for serendipity in this discipline.

Particularly in comics, the practice of sequential art is a teachable, studied skill that stems from an imaginative employment of science and language knowledge as well as the ability to portray or caricature and handle the tools of drawing.

Indeed, an average comic book story would reveal the involvement of a range of diverse disciplines that would surprise a pedagogue.

It is worth the risk of over-simplification to attempt a charting of these to make the point.

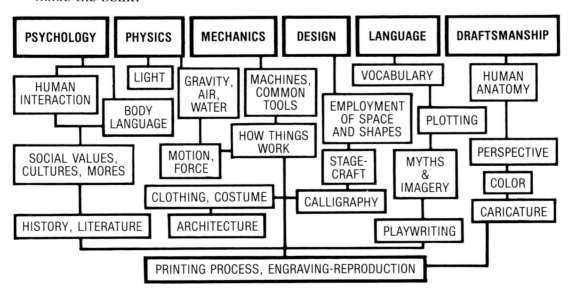

PREPARATION

A fundamental command of drawing and writing is a prerequisite. This is an art form that concerns itself with realism because it purports to tell stories. Sequential art deals with recognizable imagery. The tools are human (or animal) beings, objects and devices, natural phenomena and language. Obviously a serious study of available text books or courses in anatomy, perspective design and composition are important preparation. Each of these disciplines is a study in itself, and should be a part of the student's course of training. A steady diet of reading, particularly in the short story form, is essential to plotting and narrative skills. Reading fiction stimulates the student's imagination. In practice the artist 'imagines' for the reader. Reading also provides a useable bank of information. In an art form where the author/ artist must have at his command a wide body of quickly retrievable facts and information about innumerable subjects the input of knowledge is never ending. After all, this is an art form that deals with human experience.

HOW TO LOOK AT THINGS

How the artist 'sees' life and the objects with which he must deal lies at the heart of the skill with which he employs them. Objects, how they work and how to represent them, must be seen fundamentally in order to understand them.

Here are a few basic elements of phenomenon and imagery with which the artist must deal. They are selected out of whole universe of subjects that must be understood.

Maximum back

Maximum forward

THE HUMAN MACHINE: Consider the human (or animal) body as a mechanical device. As such, it has a limited range of movement. Understanding what it can or cannot do is critical to its manipulation.

148

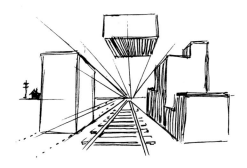

PERSPECTIVE: Distance, relationship of one shape to another, configuration and size is shown on a one-dimensional surface by the use of lines that ultimately converge upon a point on the horizon — called a 'vanishing point.'

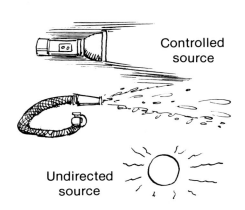

Controlled source

Undirected source

LIGHT/SHADE: Light from its source should be perceived as a flow of water. The absence of light is darkness. An object interrupting a flow of light is dark on the side facing away from it. All objects of a group under the same light source will have a side (or shadow) on the side away from it. All objects in a flow of light throw a shadow onto whatever is behind it — wall, floor or another object. Shadows conform to the surface of the shape upon which they fall. The employment of light has an emotional effect. Shadow evokes fear — light implies safety.

Controlled source

Undirected source

THE UNKNOWN

THE KNOWN

THREAT

CANDOR

149

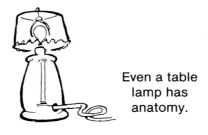

Even a table lamp has anatomy.

OBJECTS: All objects with which people live are essentially machines. From a simple empty box to an automobile they have an anatomy and a limited range of operating capability. In this they should be considered as you would a human body.

Casual props, must work accurately. For example, understand how a door is hinged.

DEVICES: Understand how they work! The reader will know how they *should* work and will respond negatively if you are inaccurate. This holds true in a realistic as well as humorously exaggerated cartoons.

The weight of an object affects the result of its response to the force of gravity.

GRAVITY: Everything on the surface of the earth responds to gravitational force. This is a phenomenon that human beings struggle with continually. Its use therefore as a story telling device is widespread and commonly understood.

Gravity-Defying Object

Soft Cloth

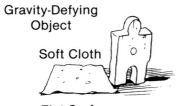

Flat Surface

DRAPERY: All cloth on an object or body responds to the vertical force of gravity! Its response to that force depends on the shape of the gravity-defying object underneath.

Pinch Points (Points on an underlying object that support cloth)

Draping Effect (Sag in cloth)

Gravity Defying Object in Motion (Pull of action helps cloth defy gravity)

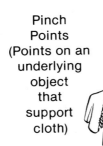

Fluting (occurs when the unsupported cloth responds to the downward pull of gravity.)

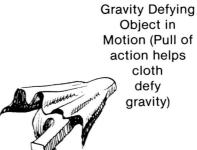

150

Cartoon rendering

Realistic rendering

Realistic rock

Cartoon rock

Each panel is a geometric shape.

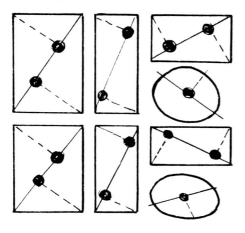

The FOCAL POINTS in any given panel occur at the point where a perpendicular line from opposite corners intersects with a diagonal from the remaining corners. These areas can be effectively used to position a vital object or action.

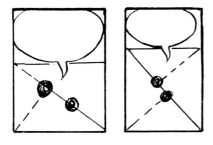

CARTOONING: The cartoon is the result of exaggeration and simplification. Realism is adherence to most of the detail. The elimination of some of the detail in an image makes it easier to digest and adds to humor. Retention of detail begets believability because it is closest to what the reader actually sees. The cartoon is a form of impressionism.

COMPOSITION: Each panel should be regarded as a stage wherein an arrangement of elements takes place. They must be arranged with a clear purpose. Nothing in a panel or page should be accidental or placed there casually. The primary consideration in composing a scene is the center of attention. The mission is to focus on the major item or action by placing it in the area of major attention. The panel is a geometric shape and has a 'focal point' which the reader's eye first engages before moving on to absorb the rest of the scene. Each panel has its own 'focal point' depending on its shape.

Where a 'balloon' dominates the major portion of a panel the remaining area is the box which becomes subject to a 'focal point.'

Caution! . . . The student should be warned that 'Focal Points' unlike the rules of perspective are employed as a 'rule-of-thumb.' The 'Points' are to be understood as 'Areas.' The selection and determination of the item or action to be placed there is a value judgment. They are an aid in the act of composing a scene.

151

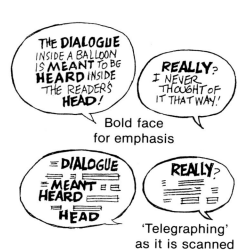

Bold face
for emphasis

'Telegraphing'
as it is scanned

SPLITTING THE BALLOON
Panel 1   Panel 2

Too much time has elapsed between panels to retain the thought.

EDITING THE BALLOON
Original   Alteration

Too many balloons for a single speech slows the action.

This editing frees the visual and so speeds the action.

BALLOONS: Think of balloons, I mean the dialogue *within,* as being repeated by the reader inside his head. Think of yourself 'acting-out' the speech out loud — for that is what the reader will do internally. Keep in mind you are dealing with sound. Emphasis is dealt with by the use of bold face. Remember that the reader's first action is to scan the page, then the panel. If the pictorial value of the images is very exciting or filled with great detail — there will be a tendency to 'skim' the balloon text. So a wise defensive stratagem is to try to deploy the bold face not only in service of sound but to 'telegraph' the message. The reader should be able to get the thrust or sense of the dialogue out of the bold-face letters alone. Avoid hyphenation — it slows reading. Don't lose sight of the fact that there is a time lapse between panels. Therefore dialogue jumping in MID-SENTENCE from panel to panel will often look inept and could make the action difficult to follow . . . or downright silly. Three or four balloons coming out of the same figure in one panel is a device I personally avoid because I think it is destructive to action flow. As a rule I would advise that the dialogue be edited down (30 words to a balloon is maximum for convenient reading) or split and placed in an added panel.

Annoyed, the man
slapped the fly on
his bald head with
his open palm

AN ILLUSTRATION

A VISUAL

VISUALS VS. ILLUSTRATION:

In comics the drawings are visuals. In textbooks they are illustrations. A visual replaces text . . . an illustration simply repeats or amplifies, decorates or sets a climate for mood. Think of your function as a visualizer rather than an *illustrator*.

TECHNOLOGY
(Print)

In modern times sequential art has found its outlet substantially in print media such as comic book magazines and newspaper strips. The practice of comics, therefore, requires one to prepare art work for it. The artist's work must be reproducible on the publisher's specifications for it is the publisher who determines the method of printing.

PRINTING

Classically, printing is the transfer of an image engraved on a plate, after it has been coated with a film of ink, onto the surface of paper. There are three basic systems.

LETTER PRESS

OFFSET

A rubber stamp is a simple example.

A fingerprint is a simple example.

ROTOGRAVURE

The ink from inside an image cut into metal, as in an etching.

REPRODUCTION VS. RENDERING

STYLE: Art work is rendered in response to the method of its reproduction. Early comic strips were drawn in simplified black line because newspapers and magazines were mostly printed by the letterpress method. Halftone (greys) engraving was crude and the screens used were very coarse. Furthermore, the line work had to be sturdy so that it could survive web press printing on the coarse surface of cheap newsprint and pulp paper. With the development of offset printing, drawing whose line was more delicate became more viable. Rotogravure printing of comics was never very widespread in American publishing and had little impact on the style of rendering comic art.

153

ENGRAVING
The image on the original art is transferred to the printing plate.

COLOR
(Hand-Separation)

ORIGINAL ART

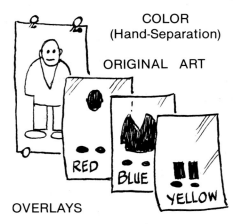

OVERLAYS

The three primary colors

Note this serves to demonstrate why line work (in comics) tended toward 'TRAPPED' lines.

Later, as color was added it was done so by the application of overlays called 'hand-separation.' The intended color was placed into each area of the art-like the 'number painting' of children's coloring books. Since color was applied by people in the engraver's plant the artist had to render his drawings so that the line work 'trapped' or provided a clearly defined containment for the color. Vignettes were, therefore, impractical.

In effect the artist was at the mercy of the people in the engraver's shop.

In modern times, with the advent of inexpensive color-process engraving by the electronic scanning method the artist can deliver a 'painting' in which he renders the color over his line work. The whole work is then *'shot'* by full color process engraving.

COLOR
(Process Separation)

ORIGINAL ART IN FULL COLOR

Filters for 3 Primary Colors

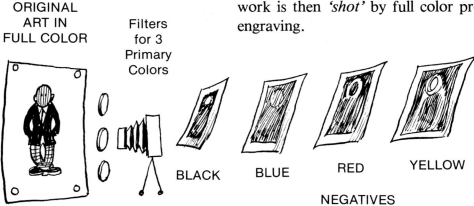

BLACK   BLUE   RED   YELLOW

NEGATIVES

154

BLUE LINE PROCESS

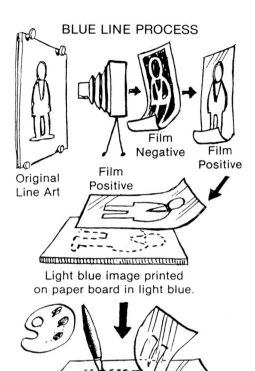

Original
Line Art

Film
Positive

Film
Negative

Film
Positive

Film Positive

Light blue image printed
on paper board in light blue.

Full color painting over
light blue image on paper board

Another method — the 'Blue Line' system, retains the integrity of line in the basic art plus the aesthetic value of a full color painting. Here the art is first prepared in line. Then it is 'shot' and printed in light blue on a paper board. The line art film is retained as a flap or overlay while a full color painting is made on the blue board. This is color separated (3-color process) and the line film is added to it as the (black) fourth color. In this method the balloons which must be in unscreened line become part of the line art film.

Regardless of the wider latitudes for rendering which more sophisticated reproduction technology offers, this medium remains a line-art form. Line rendering has a crispness of statement that is very useful in the employment of imagery as a language.

The artist should continue to think in line for the foreseeable future.

PROCESS SEPARATION

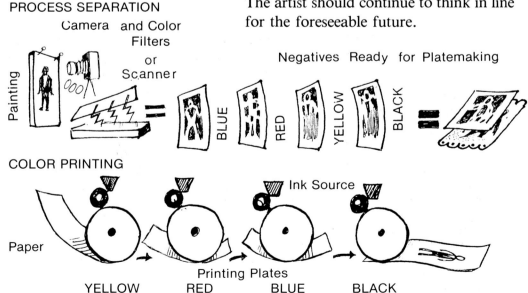

Camera and Color Filters

or

Scanner

Painting

Negatives Ready for Platemaking

BLUE   RED   YELLOW   BLACK

COLOR PRINTING

Ink Source

Paper

Printing Plates

YELLOW   RED   BLUE   BLACK

155

THE COMPUTER

Before the arrival of the computer most comics and illustration was prepared for reproduction by what in the future will be regarded as primitive process. Because of this the artist had to acquire drawing skills with the pen brush and pencil. Artwork was delivered to the printer on paper board with zip-o-tone or overlays for grey tones. This unquestionably influenced style and even the level of detail the creator was able to achieve. The computer increases the productive capacity of the creator by enabling the addition of artistic and design elements such as backgrounds, lettering and shading with only the tap of a button and the wave of a "mouse."

THE PROCESS

There are only a few general vehicles for transmitting a non-animated comic: video, computer display, internet or by print. Here we will discuss print. In modern times art for reproduction will reach the printer via computer in the following manner:

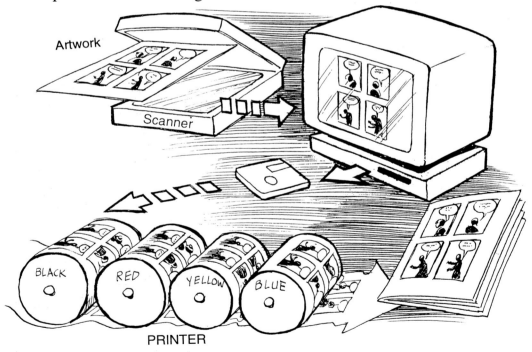

Before artwork can be used on a computer it must first be scanned. This converts it to a digital format. Artwork can also be created on a tablet which will do the same thing. To add color there are paint programs which apply color in layers and overlay the art without affecting the line art. This can be done with one overlay for all necessary color or by using several overlays, each layer can be manipulated separately.

LINE ART

LAYER 1

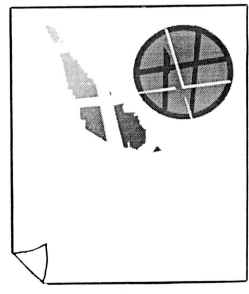

LAYER 2

LAYER 3

All of the above
is done on screen
after basic art
is scanned

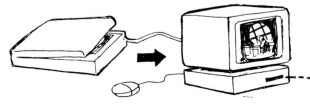

This can also be done
with a page of panels

ELECTRONIC COMICS

Historically comics were created for a page or panel or strip which are part of either a magazine or newspaper. While the flourishing of the internet as a vehicle of transmission may not necessarily replace these as a major vehicle it is certainly an alternative to print. It deserves, therefore, a consideration of how electronic capability can affect the medium. There is a certain dynamic of tactility and space in print that is very different from the 'feel' of an image on a screen. We must not lose sight of the basic fact that sequential art is a literary medium which narrates by the arrangement of images and text in an intelligible sequence. Regardless of the method of delivery the fundamental requirements of sequential art remain the same. These fundamentals are:

NARRATIVE: The "story" must adhere to a common
                  reading convention.

COMPOSITION: Panel and page must be composed for
                  narrative purposes.

CHARACTERS: The skillfull creation of "actors."

DRAFTSMANSHIP: The rendering of the elements.

As long as comics remains a medium which does not have motion, sound or dimension, the narrative process is the same.

ELECTRONIC DELIVERY

When a comic for computer screen is displayed on the screen as a page the viewer reads it in the same manner as print. So the arrangement of panels and the composing of scenes as well as balloons adheres to print rules.

Conventional reading sequence

159

Because of the "arranging" capability of this process the page layout can be experimented with so that the reading rhythm will be altered to deal with screen-reading vs. print-reading. Here is an example of "playing" with an arrangement to reach a satisfactory page layout.

There is a possibility that transmission will take the form of a panel-by-panel presentation.

This is the same comic told in an unpaneled sequence

This of course eliminates the need for the employment of the conventional panel arrangement. The traditional function of the panel as a punctuation or as an emotion-orientation no longer applies. The concentration then is on acting and composition of the scene. The posture and gesture of the actors must be more obvious to be immediately understood because the viewer will move more hurriedly from scene to scene. A conventional comic is subject to a different reading rhythm. On a print page where the reader first scans all the panels on the page, the concentration on each panel is more leisurely. But in either case the action is suggested, time is perceived and sound is implied. As the technology of transmission is improved so that images appear more quickly and the resolution is more sharp, the art will be able to be more detailed. Individual style or "art personality" as a contribution to emotional content should not be dismissed.

INDIVIDUALITY AND PERSONALITY
IN THE COMPUTER ERA

Traditionally art, its style and individuality, has been central to the personality of a comic book or strip. This generally results from a singular ability with pencil, pen or brush and has an impact on the narrative quality of the work. One might say that style is a form of imperfection.

Historically, technology has always had the effect of expanding the artists' reach while challenging their individuality. With the arrival of machines (computers) capable of generating artwork, rather than simply reproducing it, came a new impact on individuality. The old skills with the more primitive tools are being replaced by the new skills with a "mouse" or a stylus with which one draws an image while looking at a screen apart from the surface on which it is being manipulated. The creator can now mechanically produce technically perfect perspectives and geometrically accurate shapes. Thousands of color combinations which are automatically mixed and patterns of dazzling complexity can be produced by the touch of a button and they add to the creator's range. But since anyone with the same machine can do the same thing, the creator will have to go beyond a simple manipulation of a machine in order to generate images that are singular, stylistic, imperfectly individual, with personality.

All the evidence at hand indicates that personality or individuality in the practice of Sequential Art will have to come from the generation of ideas and the mastery of narrative style.

INDEX

PANEL	A box which contains a given scene. (Box, Frame.)
BORDER	The outline of the panel.
GUTTERS	The space between panels.
PAGE	A leaf of the publication or total area of work.
TIER	Row of panels (left to right) on page.
BALLOONS	The container of the text-dialogue spoken by character.
TAIL	Pointer leading from balloon to speaker.
STYLE	The manner in which artist draws.
TECHNIQUE	The manner in which art is rendered.
BIRDS EYE VIEW	The scene as seen from above it.
WORMS EYE VIEW	The scene as seen from beneath it.
GESTURE	Human movement of expression.
POSTURE	Attitude of the body.

OTHER BOOKS
BY WILL EISNER

GRAPHIC STORYTELLING

•

A CONTRACT WITH GOD

•

NEW YORK, THE BIG CITY

•

A LIFE FORCE

•

LIFE ON ANOTHER PLANET

•

WILL EISNER READER

•

THE BUILDING

•

THE DREAMER

•

CITY PEOPLE

•

WILL EISNER SKETCHBOOK

•

THE SPIRIT'S CASE BOOK

•

TO THE HEART OF THE STORM

•

INVISIBLE PEOPLE

•

DROPSIE AVENUE

•

FAMILY MATTER

•

LAST DAY IN VIETNAM

•

MINOR MIRACLES

•

NAME OF THE GAME